SMOLDER

UNDERGROUND ENCOUNTERS 1

LISA CARLISLE

LISACARLISLEBOOKS

SMOLDER

A Novella in the Underground Encounters series.

We all lead double lives in a way. Only the most trusted are allowed into our private space. When my reality and fantasy worlds collide one night, I end up in danger.

I never thought a gym crush could be deadly.

All I wanted was an escape from reality. Being a firefighter can be stressful and I unwind at an underground goth club. I can forget about being on call for danger, and just be Nike, a woman who likes to lose herself in music and dance. But when I spot the guy I fantasized about at the rock climbing gym, he discovers my secret.

Michel has a darker one and a connection to a world I never knew existed. My life is threatened and I have to choose whether to go with Michel. How do I find a way out of this nightmare that doesn't end with me getting burned— or worse, sucked dry by a vampire?

Smolder is a novella that starts the Underground Encounters series, set in a club that attracts supernatural creatures. Step into Vamps and discover a thrilling new world of steamy paranormal romance featuring sexy shifters, thirsty vampires, wicked witches, and gorgeous gargoyles.

Don't miss any new releases, giveaways, specials, or freebies! Join the VIP list and download a free read today!

www.lisacarlislebooks.com

OTHER BOOKS BY LISA CARLISLE

Underground Encounters series
Steamy paranormal romances set in a underground goth club that attracts vampires, witches, shifters, and gargoyles.

- *Smolder*
- *Fire*
- *Ignite*
- *Burn*

Chateau Seductions
An art colony on a remote New England island lures creative types—and supernatural characters. Steamy paranormal romances.

- *Darkness Rising*
- *Dark Velvet*
- *Dark Muse*
- *Dark Stranger*
- *Dark Pursuit*

Underground Encounters series
Gargoyle shifters, wolf shifters, and tree witches have divided the Isle of Stone after a great battle 25 years ago. One risk changes it all...

- *Knights of Stone: Mason*
- *Knights of Stone: Lachlan*
- *Knights of Stone: Bryce*
- *Seth: a wolf shifter romance in the series*
- *Knights of Stone: Calum*
- *Knights of Stone: Gavin (coming soon)*

Stone Sentries
Meet your perfect match the night of the super moon — or your perfect match for the night. A cop teams up with a gargoyle shifter when demons attack Boston.

- *Tempted by the Gargoyle*
- *Enticed by the Gargoyle (coming soon)*
- *Captivated by the Gargoyle (coming soon)*

Night Eagle Operations
A paranormal romantic suspense novel

- *When Darkness Whispers*

Berkano Vampires
A shared author world with dystopian paranormal romances.

OTHER BOOKS BY LISA CARLISLE

- *Immortal Resistance*

Blood Courtesans

A shared author world with the vampire blood courtesans.

- *Pursued: Mia*

Visit LisaCarlisleBooks.com to learn more!

CHAPTER 1

N*ike*

We all lead double lives, don't we? We present our public persona to most and our private lives to few, if any. Only the most trusted are ever let into our secret worlds.

Although our personalities were vastly different, Maya and I escaped reality together going to Vamps, an underground club that attracted the outcasts and welcomed them in its dark embrace. Both firefighters and the only two women at our firehouse, we forged a close friendship after we discovered a shared interest in B-horror movies and music, including rock and punk. She introduced me to the club, one I'd characterize as alternative and Goth. Although with the array of club-goers and outfits, it was difficult to classify into any one category.

It was a Saturday night, and Maya and I headed to the one place we could be ourselves. We wouldn't be called weird for dressing in freaky clothing and dancing to music never played on the Top 40. I'd hate for our male firefighting counterparts to ever find us there, yet, we all have our secrets. I'd bet they had many they wouldn't wish for us to discover as well.

The things I've seen, and wish I could unsee, in people's houses. Not just closets, but basements, attics, bedrooms…

Aren't we all freaks on the inside?

THE STRICT DRESS code at Vamps warned curious passersby away: "No jeans, no sneakers, no baseball caps. If in doubt, wear black."

I glanced at the stone gargoyles that flanked the entrance as if they were old friends. Perhaps they were built there to appear creepy and warn visitors away from this underground club. I preferred to think they signaled protection for whoever entered.

Maya pulled on the aged-bronze door handle.

"Ladies, you look ravishing as always," said Byron, the bouncer. "Like you're ready to break some hearts."

"That's the plan," I said.

"Except yours," Maya said, as she gave him a kiss on the cheek.

"You're such a flirt," Byron said. "Go on in."

"This is going to be a great night," Maya said, grabbing my arm and pulling me along. "I can feel it."

"The only thing I feel right now is your death grip."

"Sorry, Nike." She released my arm. "Maybe we'll meet someone special."

"Ha! In a club like this?" I scoffed. "Come on. I'm only here to dance, not date. You wouldn't seriously date some guy you met while wearing a tiny schoolgirl outfit, would you?"

I followed her down the dark tunnel lit by candelabra attached to the stone walls. The flames were powered by electricity, as not to violate any fire codes, yet they still emanated a fiery glow. so

"No. Ugh. Do I ever?" she asked, giving me her incredulous look. "Doesn't mean we can't meet interesting people. Remember those guys from England a few months ago? They were a blast."

"They were okay," I said, shrugging. "I don't know how they found out about this place. All I know is I'm hoping for a good night. It was such a shitty week at the firehouse, and I'm more than ready to let off some steam."

"And it's not often we get a Saturday night off. Definitely the best night of the week here."

The public would consider Vamps freaky every other night it was open as well. For some reason, Saturday was extra *special*. Maybe it was DJ Mistress Mona putting on faster, more exciting music that worked the crowd up to a dancing frenzy on the three platform stages and dance floor. Maybe the bartenders put an extra kick in their smoky concoctions. Or maybe it was the Saturday night regulars, decked out in their most outrageous and scanty outfits, who made Vamps their own.

A tingle of excitement spread over my skin. I loved coming here. It was exactly what I needed to decompress after long shifts in the firehouse—and some emotional stressors. Deaths were to be expected. Everyone died eventually. But seeing the anguish of their loves ones was tough to experience—especially when it was from a preventable tragedy. A rising number of opioid overdoses was especially troubling. I was only 24 and had responded to far too many calls of ODs with people younger than me.

We couldn't save all of them.

Still, I loved being a firefighter. I could help people—most of the time. I just needed healthy ways to cope. What worked so far was challenging myself with rock climbing in a local indoor gym. Plus, my lack of a love life was made more interesting by my crush on one of the guys who worked there.

The other way I coped was dressing up in something slinky and feminine—as far as you could get from a firefighter's uniform—and coming to Vamps. It gave me a much-needed break from my work persona. Music that wasn't mainstream had always interested me. It branded me an outcast in high school, but I'd found a tribe here where non-traditional interests were celebrated rather than scorned.

When Maya and I made it to the main dance area, the floor was packed. People were free to be themselves, wearing whatever suited them—from fishnets and corsets, steampunk to punk rock—in an environment where they could be uninhibited and unjudged. And they wore black. Lots of it.

I often asked where the regulars came from. The club seemed like it would fit better in downtown Boston or at least eclectic Salem rather than this little artists' village tucked in the North Shore. Most of the regulars came from Gloucester, Salem, Portsmouth, and some even drove up from Boston. They attributed it to a more authentic local flavor than the city clubs often frequented by gawking tourists looking for a freak show.

Maya and I slinked our way through the dance floor. The crowd pulsated around us in an orgy of black, leather and skintight vinyl while gargoyle statues stared down upon them from their protective perches on the walls. Maya and I maneuvered into an empty space and were entranced by the crowd's energy, dancing to the beat.

A remix of Rob Zombie's *Living Dead Girl* came on. Even though I didn't have a drink, I lost myself in the music, trying to shake off work-mode. When a couple of guys danced with us, I barely noticed and didn't mind.

Maya and I would dance with them, maybe have a drink, but we'd never give out our numbers. Besides, how do you interact over coffee with some guy you met who had been wearing leather pants, chains and boots that gave a new definition to the word *stomp*?

After a few more songs, I said, "Come on, Maya, let's get a drink."

"Hey, where are you ladies going?"

"We'll see you later," Maya said, and she took my hand to try to move our way off the dance floor.

One of the guys must have grabbed her arm as she yanked me back with her. Uh oh. This was unusual. The guys weren't usually pushy here, so we got away without protest. Unlike some of the other clubs on the North Shore or Boston where you'd be hit on repeatedly by drunk townies or college jocks.

"Don't leave," one of the guys said to Maya. He had a swarthy complexion and had to be close to six-feet tall. The grim look on his face vanished as he replaced it with a smile he probably thought looked charming. I found it creepy. "I like dancing with you."

"Maybe later," Maya said with a smile.

Maya was sweet. She never wanted to hurt anyone's feelings, which was one of the things I loved about her, but also made me warier than I typically was. I had to watch out for her because she'd look out for others before herself.

"Fine. I'll buy you a drink."

The guy wasn't giving up yet, was he? I paused to assess the situation. Would he leave her alone, or would this escalate? Before I could gauge this guy's level of soberness, his friend stepped before me. Oh great. The other guy's assertiveness must have encouraged him.

"Yeah, we're all having a good time," his friend said.

The friend trailed his fingers over my bare shoulder and over my arm in a way that made me leery. It was like ants crawling over my skin.

I grabbed his hand and pulled it off me. "That's too personal to touch someone like that who you don't know."

He laughed. "I'm trying to get to know you."

"Now it's *definitely* not happening." I then addressed the first guy. "Let go of her."

He narrowed his eyes at me. "She's able to make her own decisions."

I turned to Maya. "Do you want to hang out with this dude?"

Her eyes widened, screaming *hell no*. "I was hoping you and I could get a drink, take a little break." Her voice came out gentler.

Maya. Got to love her. She still didn't want to hurt the guy's feelings. I didn't give a crap. They'd evolved from minor annoyances to pains in the ass.

I glared at the guy. Despite my high-heeled boots, I still had to look up. "She's all set." Where was the nearest bouncer? If this escalated, I'd have to signal for one. But no way was I breaking eye contact. That might fuel this guy's desire to dominate.

The guy scowled and muttered something as he turned away. After I exhaled, I took Maya's hand and steered her through the crowd. We squeezed through dancers to make our way to the darkly lit bar guarded by more stone gargoyles on each end. My heart pounded even after we'd created some distance. I turned back to make sure we weren't being followed, but the guys had already creeped up behind some other women, doing that leery dance that I hated. What did they think, if they got within two inches of pressing their crotch against a woman's ass, they'd win a free pass letting them in?

"Thanks, Nike," Maya said as we made it to the other side of the dance floor. "You know how I hate being mean."

"I'm just impatient," I said. "You would have given him a piece of your mind if he pushed you enough."

She shook her head. "Some guys…"

While we approached the bar, I felt the burn of someone staring at me.

Oh no, it wasn't one of those guys again, was it?

I glanced around.

It was him. Looking amazing in a black leather jacket.

Holy shit. *He* was here. My gym crush. All that adrenaline that had pumped through me moments before while dealing with the pushy jerks vanished.

In all the times I'd come here, dressed in miniscule outfits, never had I felt so exposed. I wished I wasn't wearing such a tight laced-up black leather dress that exposed a lot of cleavage.

He was sitting on one of the dark-red leather stools, facing the crowd. I caught his eye and turned away. Those ice-blue eyes were so penetrating. Each time I'd met his gaze at the rock climbing gym, I'd have the same reaction, averted his gaze.

Why didn't I have the guts to converse beyond simple hellos? He was just another guy, so why did he have that effect upon me? There were tons of hot guys with jacked bodies at the gym. This one—*only this one*—made me react this way, like a turntable that had gotten stuck. Something about him was different, putting him far out of my league.

My palms heated and I grew aware of the sound of my heartbeat despite the reverberation of the pounding bass around us.

"I know you from the gym, don't I?"

Oh God. Whenever I heard that sultry voice and the accent, I trembled slightly inside. Was there anything sexier than a French accent? During my brief semester in the south of France my junior year of college, I was in a constant state of sexual arousal with sounds of the language all around me. Especially when purred by hot men.

I opened my mouth to answer, but nothing came out. Maya elbowed me.

"Ye-yes," I stammered, trying to sound nonchalant. "I go to Rock Hard Climbing. I've, uh, seen you there. You belayed me once."

His eyes gleamed. "I remember."

"I'll catch up with you later." Maya scooted to an empty spot at the other end of the red-and-black-marbled bar.

Damn it. How could she leave me alone with him? She must have figured out he was the guy I drooled about when I clammed up like an idiot.

I stared at Maya as she scanned the crowd on the dance floor, shooting invisible daggers at her back. *I'm going to kill her later.*

In all those months fantasizing about this guy, never did I think it would start as awkward as this. Perhaps a friendly hello would evolve into a deeper conversation. I'd seem aloof at first, but he'd say something funny to break through my exterior. Things would progress nice and slow until he finally asked me out.

He snapped me out of my thoughts when he said, "I knew I recognized you. But you look," he paused, "different."

Never, *never*, did I think we'd have a conversation in some underground club. All while my breasts were pushed up against a leather laced-up bodice, accentuated by a brooch with a silhouetted skull.

"Um, yes." I peered up at him. He wore a tight black T-shirt that enhanced rather than hid all those hours he put in rock climbing. His black jeans were tight and I didn't dare look to see if they enhanced certain areas as well. "You look different, too, out of gym clothes."

He chuckled. Did I say something funny? I didn't think so.

"I only wear my gym clothes while I'm working. But I guess that's the only time you'd see me," he said.

I smiled. If only there were other times.

"I'm Michel," he said, pronouncing it with French accentuation on the syllables. Damn, that was hot. He put out his hand.

"*Mee-shell,*" I repeated softly the way he had said it, letting his name roll over my tongue like a smooth whiskey. "I'm Nike," I answered, shaking his hand.

The touch of his skin arrested me and I hoped he didn't catch my quick intake of breath.

"Like the goddess of victory," he said. "Fitting. I've seen you conquer many tough climbs."

He held on to my hand for a few seconds longer than what was customary and lightly ran his thumb across my knuckles. My skin tingled with heat where he'd touched it and I resisted closing my eyes to revel in the sensation. I tried not to let his remark go to my head and set my fantasies in motion again, but that slight caress made it inevitable.

I pushed away a vision of us in bed together, rolling in satin sheets as I whispered his name through hot, passionate kisses. *He's just being polite,* I told myself. He'd do the same to anyone else he recognized from the gym.

"Yes. Thank you. Most people say, 'Like the sneakers?' My mother was into Greek mythology."

"I see," he said. "Ni-kee," he drew out the syllables in a low rasp.

Hearing him say my name with his accent excited me.

"Can I get you a drink?"

My heart began beating faster again. A drink meant I'd be talking to him a bit longer. This was better, yet faster, than any fantasy I had concocted on my own slow timeline.

"Yes, please. I'd love the Sepulchre by the Sea." Many of Vamps' specialty drinks gave a nod to classic literature, especially Edgar Allan Poe.

"Nice choice," he said. "I'm keen on the Dorian Gray."

"Well then, may you never age."

He gazed off into the distance with an odd smile. "Yet his soul paid the price."

As he turned to the bartender, I stole a glance at his profile. His features were so chiseled, as if carved from granite. His sandy-brown hair fell slightly past his chin, long enough to give him a devil-may-care look. I admired the tapered cheekbones, the strong jawline, and the rough stubble.

How many times had I imagined myself reaching out and stroking his jawline, letting the coarse stubble lightly caress my fingertips? The contrast of it against the sensitive skin as he kissed my lips. As he kissed down my neck, down to my breasts, tickling and teasing my nipples, kissing down the front of my body, driving me wild with soft kisses and the roughness of his cheek against my skin.

I didn't know his name, so I would make one up in my fantasies of the two of us together. Johnny, maybe. Jake. Names from the hot guys in the eighties movies I loved. But Michel was even better. So French. So cool. *Michel.*

He handed me my drink. Now at least I would have something to do with my hands. The bartender lingered in front of Michel although she had plenty of customers vying to get her attention, waving twenties. With her tight red leather corset and pink bob, she was definitely dressed to be noticed.

He wasn't paying any attention to this scarlet vixen's embellished assets. He was watching me with those eyes. *Those eyes.* So intense I could barely breathe.

"Do you need anything else, Michel?" she interrupted,

leaning forward to display her breasts even more advantageously, if that was possible.

"Thank you, Tracy. That'll be all," he said.

Tracy retreated her twin girls off the bar, pouted slightly and went back to tend to other customers.

"Do you know her?" I asked.

"Yes," he said.

That was it? I didn't want to pry, but didn't want to flirt with some girl's honey right in front of her either.

When he didn't elaborate, I asked, I hoped sounding nonchalant, "Are you two involved?"

"*Mon Dieu, non.*"

I hid a smile of relief by taking a sip of my drink. Why did I ask that anyway? She was a bartender and they knew each other's names. Big deal. But there was definitely some sort of familiarity between them.

"So, Nike, what else do you do besides rock climb and dance at Vamps? I have to admit, I'm surprised to see you in a club like this."

What did he mean by that? I didn't seem like the Vamps type? He probably thought I was too prudish to come here since I was so shy around him at the gym.

"I'm a firefighter," I answered, noticing he bristled almost imperceptibly.

Yes, you're tough, I reminded myself. *An independent woman who would not be intimidated in this situation. Sure, he's starred in a number of your fantasies, but that's just it—a fantasy. Maybe he's a jerk in real life. Get a grip.*

"A firefighter?" he repeated, stroking his chin stubble. "Interesting." He smiled slightly as if at his own private joke. "Are you here looking to put out some fires?"

"Off-duty," I answered. "Maya and I worked a long shift earlier. Dancing is a good way to get rid of the excess energy.

Otherwise I'd just toss and turn in bed all night no matter how tired I was."

Stop babbling, Nike! Time to shut up.

He reached out and brushed his fingertips across the top of my hand. "Tossing and turning in bed isn't so bad," he said, "if you're with the right person."

Before I could censor myself, I blurted, "I guess I haven't found the right person, but maybe my luck will change." I dared looking in those cool blue eyes and raised an eyebrow. Had I gone from being tongue-tied around him to flirting? Not my strong suit. I suppose that was progress.

"Nike, I've often wondered about you. You're in the gym all the time, but you keep to yourself. Many people go there to socialize first and work out second."

Uh-oh, did he think I was some freak? Or rude? It was a cruel irony when people interpreted shyness as bitchiness. I wasn't like Maya and couldn't strike up a conversation with everyone. I tended to listen more than talk; watch and assess. Funny, that Michel didn't realize one of the reasons I was there so often was once I knew he was in the vicinity, I found it hard to leave.

"You intrigue me," he continued. He lifted his hand to my face and barely grazed his knuckles across my cheek. My skin burned again under his cool touch and my cheeks warmed.

He leaned forward and whispered in my ear. "I'd love to get to know you better."

Parts of my body that had been dormant for many months suddenly reawakened as his warm breath caressed my ear.

"Would you like to talk somewhere where we can have a little more privacy? We can go to a room upstairs."

Oh mama! All I wanted to do was jump into his lap right

there and put my arms around his neck. At that moment, I didn't care who else was around me. All I wanted was him.

I took a few deep yoga breaths to slow my raging heartbeat and regain my composure. "Would you excuse me for a minute?"

"Of course," he said. "I hope you come right back."

I smiled to indicate I planned on it and tried to walk slowly and seductively on my way to the ladies' room. It wasn't fthe fire with the high-heeled lace-up boots. You either strutted sexily in them or you tripped and fell on your ass. No middle ground.

Luckily, I made it across the crowd without falling, so I hoped the sexy quotient was kicking up in high gear. When I turned back, he was still watching me. I gave what I hoped was a seductive *be right back* smile and then scanned the crowd for Maya.

She was wearing a schoolgirl outfit with a short blue plaid skirt and tight white tank top. Unfortunately, she wasn't the only naughty schoolgirl on the dance floor tonight, which made it more difficult. Since most of the crowd was wearing black, I only had to scan the more colorfully dressed women.

Bingo. She was with some tall guy who looked an awful lot like Trent Reznor. She seemed quite lost in the music, dancing to *Black No. 1* by Type O Negative, one of her favorite bands. The guy seemed to be just as into it, more focused on his moves than hitting on her.

Maya glanced over at where she'd last seen me with Michel and then glanced around. I raised my hand to catch her attention. She whispered something to fake Trent. He nodded and she walked toward me.

In the ladies' room, I waited. And breathed. I tried more deep yoga inhales through the nose and exhales through the mouth to try to slow my heartbeat.

Maya burst in. "That's the guy, isn't it? The one who looks like Bradley Cooper in *The Hangover*?"

"Yes," I said.

"I knew it," she hollered. "I could tell when he mentioned the gym and you turned into a blithering idiot."

"Thanks for noticing."

"Man, I should go out there and tell him he's the reason you look so hot in that sexy dress. Look at those shoulders," she said. "Sexy as hell. I'd kill to have those. And I know one thing. You wouldn't have spent so much time rock climbing without being distracted by that eye candy." She walked toward the door.

"Maya!" I shouted. "Don't!"

"I'm kidding, Nike. What the heck happened out there?" she asked.

"He asked me to go upstairs with him to a room. I'm debating what to do."

Maya's eyes widened in a look between shock and confusion. "What are you, nuts? The guy you've wanted for oh-I-don't-know-how-long and have been too chicken-shit to talk to just happens to be here *and* just happens to ask you to be alone with him *and* you're debating it in the ladies' room with me?"

"Well, what the hell am I supposed to do? Jump him?"

"If you want," Maya said. "God, Nike, for some kick-ass chick during the day, you sure get strange when it comes to this guy. Since when do you care what some guy thinks of you? You work in a firehouse full of guys and stand your own."

"He's different," I said.

"Different how?"

"I don't know. But he's not like the other guys."

"Have you ever talked to him before tonight?"

"Sort of."

"Meaning?"

"Well, just gym hellos, you know. And he belayed me once."

"Is that rock climbing lingo? Because I have no idea what it means." She wiggled her eyebrows. "I hope it's sexual."

I snorted. Only Maya. "It's not. It means he held the rope as I climbed. He gave me a hand when I didn't have a partner. I'm surprised I didn't lose all control of my limbs and dangle mid-air."

Maya laughed. "I'm picturing it."

"Shut up, it's not funny."

Still grinning, she said, "Oh, but it is." She planted her hands on her hips. "Come on. I've seen you take men and turn them into jelly before leaving them hanging with their mouths open. You probably would have kicked those guys' asses earlier if they didn't back off. How can some guy you've barely spoken to leave you all tongue-tied?"

I sighed. It was a bit dramatic, but hell, nothing about this situation made me feel like myself. "I wish I knew."

"Listen to me, Nike. And listen good. You want this guy. You've wanted this guy for a long time. He wants you, too, or he wouldn't have asked you to go with him. I don't know what you're afraid of, but think of your theme song and get out there."

When Maya first met me, she said I had a bad ass theme song with the Misfits song *Nike-a-Go-Go.* Discovering she had good taste in music, we hit it off. Since then, she'd play my "theme" when I needed a kick in the ass to spur me into action.

"Nobody's saying you have to sleep with the guy," she added. "Nobody's saying you'll run off and marry him either. Who the hell knows what's going to happen, but neither of us will find out hanging out in here. Just go out there and *see what the fuck happens.*"

CHAPTER 2

Michel
Quel con, stop acting like an ass. You're coming on too strong. You'll scare her away.

I sipped my drink as I watched her walk away. God, her ass was sexy. Here tonight, her dress showed what a hot body she had.

A firefighter? It made things a bit more interesting since fire was one of the few things that could harm me. In fact, it was one of the few things that terrified me, reminding me of the horrid past when I'd been turned. She made her living combating what I feared. I could never tell her this. If she found out the truth about me, she'd run.

That is *if* she came back.

I glanced at the gargoyle statues perched around the room. They saw much more than they let on. I'd brought them here as guards. Vamps attracted more than humans, luring supernatural creatures, which could be dangerous. I'd created the club as an outlet for those who were different, like myself, once I'd gotten past the moping stage of my unnatural existence. We didn't all fit in with what most might consider normal. Nor did we want to be.

Yes, I acknowledged the gargoyles, if they were watching me in silent, amusement. *I might have blown it.*

Why did I ask her to go into a private room with me within the first ten minutes of us talking? She might think I'm some lech trying to get a piece of action. Why would she think otherwise? She didn't know me at all, aside from brief exchanges at my gym. I might greet her as I would any other client or compliment her technique, but there was always an underlying element to the words that made them mean more than the superficial greetings to others in passing. She intrigued me, and my interest grew with each passing week.

I worried I'd crossed the line with the way I couldn't tear my eyes from her. She wasn't a natural talent at rock climbing, but pushed herself with increasingly more difficult challenges. Considering my supernatural abilities, I had an unfair advantage, so I might not be the most impartial observer. I loved to climb, to find a challenging route to tackle and conquer, to find the proper strategy to do so. She appeared to share the same spirit for it as she came two or three times a week. I admired her tenacity—as well as the more aesthetic aspects of her body.

Fortunately, she was often absorbed in whatever climb she'd chosen to tackle, but still, sometimes she'd caught me staring. And when our eyes met, unmistakable heat would rip through me. We'd barely spoken more than a few sentences the entire time I'd known her, but something about her got to me. She was *right there*, yet so unattainable.

Once, I had the opportunity to belay her when one of her regular partners went into the locker room. What a lovely memory. Watching her from that angle from below. Seeing her lithe body maneuver up the wall. Having a damn good reason to stare at her ass.

Merde, that image tormented me many nights when I was alone in my bed.

Something else about that one opportunity struck me with a more personal chord. In those moments, she'd put her trust in me to support and protect her. Something I wished to repeat, yet I hadn't offered a helping hand since. I hadn't found the right opportunity when she was without a partner.

Even more enjoyable than her gym visits was when she came to Vamps on a weekend. She often appeared reserved and a bit self-conscious at first, but then would loosen up when she danced. How I loved to see the joy spread on her face, the way she moved her body...

I loved to watch her enjoy herself.

In truth, I'd like to enjoy myself with her.

It wouldn't be right. My situation made it impossible to have a relationship with a human like her. Inevitably, it would have to end.

But perhaps we could be lovers for a short time.

"Can I get you anything else, Michel?"

Tracy's interruption broke my train of thought. She was a bartender who had been trying to get my attention for months.

"No thanks, Tracy."

She was beautiful, but she didn't do it for me. Half the guys in the club would kill to go home with her tonight. But she didn't have an allure the way Nike did.

What made Nike so intriguing? She always seemed focused at the rock climbing gym. Women who had been climbing there for years and knew exactly what they were doing, would feign sudden ignorance to spark a conversation with a question. But not Nike.

Seeing her up close tonight made it all the harder not to think about her. The skintight dress was torturous. How could I look and not want to touch her? Her breasts were displayed to their best advantage in a revealing bodice. And I already paid close attention to how closely the dress stretched over her ass. *Merde*, I grew hard thinking about her.

My mind entertained a vision of her tonight looking so deliciously vampish. Her auburn hair fell loose in long waves, no longer tied back in a tight ponytail. I inhaled again, remembering the floral scent I picked up when whispering in her ear. And the light, sweet scent of her blood. The innocent yet sensual combination would haunt me for a long time.

At the gym, her face was usually scrubbed clean of all makeup, but tonight it was artfully made up. Her lips outlined in a dark-red hue that added to the gothic allure. Her eyes. Yes, her eyes framed by her long, dark lashes. She looked exotic and sensuous.

In the gym, I thought her eyes were a kind of blue, but here in the darkly lit club, they radiated a jade green. Did she have a hazel color that changed according to what she wore, or her mood? Mysterious, like her. What would they look like when she was making love, full of passion and desire? A vision of us naked, making love in my loft, entered my mind and I closed my eyes for a moment to linger in the fantasy.

Nike. Definitely a goddess.

A few minutes later, Nike passed with her friend in the crowd. Her friend walked away and Nike turned back in my direction.

She was coming back—*to me*. I bet every guy would love to switch places with me right now.

I regretfully pushed the sensual images out of my mind and then dismissed the regret. What did I need the fantasy for when the real Nike was here with me?

"Hi."

"You're back."

"Yes." She shuffled on her stiletto boots. "I'm back."

"Would you like another drink?" I asked.

"No thanks. I'm fine."

"Would you like to go upstairs with me, so we can have some privacy?"

"Yes," she said, almost breathlessly, which made my cock stiffen.

I took her hand and led her toward a door in the back of the club. I used my key to open the door and lead her upstairs to my office.

"You have a key?" she asked. "How often do you come here?"

"Often. I need to check up on it. Make sure everything is going smoothly."

"You do? Why?"

"It's my club, Nike."

Nike

It's his club? How often had I come here dancing in some sexy outfit, far different from my bland gym attire, and not seen him?

"I haven't seen you here before," I said.

He led me up to another black door, which he opened with another key. The room had a desk on one side and a black sofa on the other. I was both disappointed and relieved there wasn't a bed in there.

"Oh, I've seen you." He removed his jacket and hung it on a hook behind the door. "Plenty of times."

I tried not to think of any of the slutty outfits I'd worn or sexy dance moves I might have done with any number of random guys.

He brought me to the sofa and we sat down.

"You know I don't go home with guys I meet here," I said. "I'm not like that."

"I know."

I bit my bottom lip and wondered why I'd never noticed him before. Maybe I was too busy working the dance floor.

"Why do you work at the rock climbing gym then?"

"I own it, too," he said.

Jeez, he didn't look over thirty and was already so successful. When I looked up, I noticed he had moved even closer. Our thighs were touching. I wanted to move away, uncomfortable with the sensation, yet paralyzed as I didn't want it to end.

"Don't you ever sleep?" I asked.

"Often during the day. I'm only in the gym during the week, usually evenings. And then on the weekends I sometimes come here."

He reached up and gently touched my cheek. It felt like my skin burned under his touch. I glanced into his piercing eyes and couldn't look away.

"Do you own anything else?"

His eyes focused on my lips, which made it hard for me to concentrate.

"Yes. I invest in real estate and commercial properties. It keeps me busy. But, my favorite ventures are the gym and this club. Everyone needs a chance for recreation, to escape their everyday world. And with Vamps, those of us who don't quite fit have a place where we can be ourselves."

Hot damn. He didn't seem old enough to be such a real estate mogul. I'd venture thirty-five at most. "My favorite place to escape, actually."

He ran his finger down my cheek, running it over my bottom lip. "I don't want to talk about business right now. Not when I'm thinking about you."

I sucked in a breath. Was I imagining him saying this? Another one of my crazy fantasies?

His lips barely grazed mine before he pulled away, leaving no doubt that it was real. A flood of sensations rushed through my body, ones I hadn't felt in a long time. Perhaps ever.

When he pressed his lips against mine, I responded almost involuntarily, my body reaching out for more. Perhaps I shouldn't respond with such eagerness, but I couldn't help myself.

He kissed me deeper, his tongue tasting my lower lip. I should have stopped but—but I couldn't think of why. I pressed myself against him, arching my back under his touch, giving him a subtle invitation to continue.

When he pulled away, I felt an immense sense of loss.

"I have a confession."

My heart sank. It had to be too good to be true. It happened so quickly and I responded too eagerly. "You're married, right?"

"No," he said. "Nothing like that. It's about you."

"Me?"

"I'm usually up here in my office. Behind the curtain is a two-way mirror where I can see down into the club. I've watched you from up here."

My heart beat faster for more reasons than I could count. If any other guy had said this to me, I would have pegged him a stalker, a weirdo, a creep and told him to fuck off. But since it was Michel, it was none of those things. A delicious tremor ran through my body, settling in my core.

I didn't know what to say besides "Why?" And why did this guy leave me so tongue-tied?

"I like watching you dance. I find you," he paused as if looking for the right word, "*fascinante.*"

He stroked the stubble on his chiseled chin and my eyes drew down toward the sexy cleft. A chin a sexy feature?

Since when? I never noticed a guy's chin unless it was strikingly different from the norm. Michel had a way of exuding sexiness from just about every pore, alighting all my senses to fire up with awareness.

"Yes, fascinating," he continued. "The more I've seen you, the more I wanted to get to know you. I came down to the bar when I saw you and your friend come in. I was hoping to talk to you. You give off a *don't talk to me* vibe in the gym, so focused on your climb, or belaying some lucky partner."

Shit. Guilty. Maybe I should've been less focused and more flirtatious. "Yes, well, you know… that's why I go there and all."

Ah crap, as soon as the words fell out of my mouth, I wished I could replace them with something zippier.

Michel's eyes twinkled. "How serendipitous that you approached the bar near where I was sitting."

Lucky for me, indeed.

"But I didn't imagine we'd be up here like this so soon. If I'm coming on too strong, I'll back off."

I took a deep breath to clear my mind. Reason told me to cool it, be coy, play hard to get. I'd perfected that act in the two years I'd been coming to this club since I'd turned twenty-two. However, it was difficult to find reason, let alone think clearly, with so many physical and emotional responses firing through me and clouding my senses.

Fuck it. It was time to take a bold step forward and go for what I wanted.

"No. Don't back off, please. I…um…I've been attracted to you for a long time." *Focus. Go for what you want.* "I didn't know how to express it." I leaned forward and kissed him, following passion rather than reason. "But I'm learning."

Michel's eyes took on a decadent gleam. "You're a remarkable learner."

He deepened the kiss, which quickly grew hungrier and more intense. He ran his hands down along my sides and then up to my breasts. When he thumbed over my nipple, I moaned softly, shuddering with pleasure under his gentle touch. God, I wanted more. Much more.

He gently laid me back against the sofa and lowered himself onto me, with a clear erection. Wrapping my arms around his back, I pulled him closer.

He moaned and whispered, "You're so beautiful. I wanted you for a long time, Nike."

Never had I wanted a man so much. How long had it been since I felt like this? How long had it been since I had a lover? Six months? No, closer to nine.

Yet, I'd never wanted anyone with this sort of urgency.

I swallowed and admitted, "I want you, too."

A wild rush of desire flooded me. It felt so good to feel like a woman again. He brought out sensations that made me aware that I was female, flesh and blood, stirring primal, animalistic urges.

"Please. Now," I whispered. "I don't care if it's too soon. Or if it's wrong. I want you. And I can't wait any longer."

"Me neither, *ma belle*."

A tremendous bang rocked the club and bright, flashing colors filled the room. Damn, was it my body reacting to Michel's touch with an explosive response?

No. hell no. Much worse. A gaping hole pierced the wall near his desk and the glow of streetlights shined through. Papers scattered as if swirled up by a tornado. Dust and debris rained into the room.

Michel jumped up and ran toward what was once a wall with a window.

Startled from my haze of lust, I quickly recovered. My years as a firefighter snapped me into action.

"Michel, back up. It's not safe."

He stayed where he was. I ran over to him, avoiding the shattered glass that covered the floor like an unwelcome mat. Grabbing his arm, I pulled him back, but he didn't budge. Two men dressed in black stalked like menacing, feral cats in the alley below.

"I've been looking for you, Michel," the larger one said, in a French accent similar to Michel's, but menacing rather than sexy. "Come out and play."

Michel bared teeth and snarled an animalistic growl. Only those weren't teeth, I saw. They were fangs.

Fangs! What the ever-loving fuck was that all about?

"You want to do it like *this*, Ricard," he growled, motioning to the debris falling out the window.

Oh my God. This isn't real.

Michel turned toward me. "Nike, get away from here. Go find someplace safe."

"What about you?" I asked and then looked down at those imposing figures below. "Let's get the hell away from here."

"I can't, *chérie*. Unfinished business."

In a movement almost too quick for me to register, Michel ran forward and jumped right through the hole and into the night.

I gasped and ran to the window. He descended the two stories to the pavement below, and then landed unharmed on the balls of his feet, just like a cat. How the fuck did he do that?

The larger guy hissed and went after Michel.

That's when I was hit by a cloud of smoke from below. Holding my breath, I ran back into the room. A fire started below where there were hundreds of people jammed into the club.

I grabbed a Rock Hard Climbing T-shirt from a chair and covered my nose and mouth with it as I ran out into the stairwell. Seeing the stairs were clear, I rushed down them as fast as I could in my stiletto heels, wishing I wore something faster and more functional.

Pushing open the black door back into the club, I walked into pandemonium.

CHAPTER 3

M *ichel*

Ricard had found me. After decades of this cat and mouse bullshit, he'd struck a low blow by striking in this manner. An explosion causing a fire? A fire had destroyed our village centuries ago, haunting us both with those we'd lost.

Back during that time when we were both forced into darkness.

Merde. Ricard had ruined what could have been a perfect night. In one moment, I was kissing the woman I'd wanted for so long. The next, my former comrade blew up both my fantasy and my club. *Putain.* Now I was on the cold streets of a New England night rather than in the arms of a sultry woman.

"I told you I would find you one day," Ricard said, staring me down on the empty street. "And finally make you pay."

I circled my old comrade, awaiting his next move. Time hadn't served him well. He appeared as disheveled as if he'd still lived in a bygone era, lacking the conveniences of modern times. Over two centuries ago, we'd served together,

LISA CARLISLE

and he still hunted me in vengeance for something I could not change.

"You still blame me for her death?" I demanded. "I've explained many times before."

"It doesn't change anything. It doesn't bring her back!"

"I lost someone, too. War takes something from us all. How many more lives must we lose before you move on?"

Where was Nike? She had to get away from this situation and find safety. I glanced over my shoulder to the blown-out wall of the club. A mistake. It set off Ricard's senses.

"You care about someone in there. I can feel it." He sniffed the air. "I can smell her on you. She smells delicious."

I growled at him.

Ricard gave me a caustic smile, appearing to relish my reaction. "Perhaps if I go in there and take her life, it will make me feel better about my Marie?"

When he threatened Nike, it triggered a fury within that I hadn't felt since my days on the battlefield. A time when nothing else mattered but combatting your enemy. Within a heartbeat, my world simplified into two options—fight or die. With two nightwalkers attacking my club in an effort to destroy me, the city street became the modern battleground. With a howl, I leaped onto Ricard. I'd tear him limb from limb before he could mar Nike with his indecent touch.

The other vampire, whoever he was, jumped into the mêlée. The three of us rolled on the ground, throwing vicious punches, and slamming flesh against the unrelenting concrete, all while gnashing fangs to land a fatal blow.

And with two against one, the odds were not in my favor.

Nike

My heart thudded as I surveyed the madness. Part of the back wall was blown out and a fire spread along a small bar in the back. I pinpointed the lights signaling the emergency exits.

When I'd left the room not so long ago, the vibe was relaxed. People sipped their drinks, talked or flirted, or let loose on the dance floor. Now they screamed as the fire alarms sounded and pushed one another in panic.

Fire instigated a unique form of pandemonium. The bright flash and intense heat broadcasted a dire warning— Run! Yet the smoke was often more dangerous, an insidious creeper that could sneak up and claim a victim.

An incident with pyrotechnics at a Great White show in Providence in the not too distant past served as a stark reminder of how quickly a club fire could spiral out of control. One hundred people had died. Decades earlier, the deadliest nightclub in the U.S. occurred at the Coconut Grove club in Boston. Not too many people remembered the details of that one, but local firefighters knew the details. Almost five hundred people had died. I'd never encountered a fire like the one here at Vamps with many people packed into a tight space. My priority was getting them out safely.

"Everybody stay calm and make your way to the exits," I said, pointing them out. The last thing we needed was a stampede.

If anyone heard me, they didn't take notice.

"Don't push. Just move to the exits," I shouted.

The frantic club goers bumbled over one another, not knowing where to go.

I jumped on the bar near where I had met Michel not too much earlier. Then I gave an ear-piercing whistle such as I hadn't done since I was a teenager.

This caught the attention of a few people closest to me.

"Listen up. Head to those exits," I said, pointing to the ones at the front of the club, farthest from the fire. "Move quickly, but don't push and don't panic."

While a few of the clubgoers started moving toward the exits, I guided them by pointing in the right direction. The more people who followed, the more the crowd seemed to move with them rather than in freakish circles like directionally challenged ants.

A grey shadow darted above me. What the hell was that? For some peculiar reason, I glanced at the gargoyle statues. They stood looming in their stone forms. It must have been a trick of the smoke. Or, I was losing my mind.

Maya appeared in the crowd below me. "The fire's spreading. We have to get people out fast."

I followed Maya, staying low and covering my face with the shirt to avoid smoke. Though I'd entered buildings to fight fires many times in the past, I always had my mask and gear. Here I was baring an awful lot of skin in a little dress. I felt naked. Although not so exposed as when I first spoke to Michel earlier that evening. It had only been a short while ago, yet now it seemed like ages.

Who were those guys and why did they do this?

No time to speculate. I worked with Maya to direct a panicky, arguing couple towards an exit. We had worked together for so long we didn't need words to communicate. They'd clearly had a few drinks and were freaking out. Alcohol and tense situations didn't mix well.

The heat from the growing flames reminded me of the sensation in a sauna when you're in there too long and suddenly want out. Although in a sauna, you're meant to relax, now I was focused on survival. What about Michel? Was he facing those two men on the other side of the flames? I wanted to run out to make sure Michel was okay, but my years of training won out. I'd have to get these people out to safety first.

We ran back to help others toward the exits and shouted into the bathrooms in case there were stragglers. Even if they'd heard the alarms, there was no guarantee they'd react. It amazed me how many people ignored fire alarms, thinking they were tests or false alarms.

Most of the crowd had moved outside, yet about a dozen people remained, creating a bottleneck as they tried to push through at the same time.

"One at a time," I shouted.

"Quickly, let's go!" Maya added.

The promise of fresh air outside called to me and I resisted the survival instinct to rush to it. I willed myself against the survival instincts and scoured the club to make sure nobody was stuck in there.

"I'm right with you," Maya said, catching up.

Although we'd helped people out of house fires many times before, we'd never done so in constricting clothing and spiked heels. It was surreal, almost like we were in a fire-fighter's nightmare—trying to save people without any of the equipment that would help us survive. Luckily, adrenaline provided the motivation needed to continue back to help ensure everyone escaped safely.

"Let's check behind the bars." That seemed the most obvious place to search next. When people panicked, they acted strangely. Some might cower and hide in the oddest places.

We searched and found nobody, but the flames were spreading. What was once confined to one section of the back wall was now a panorama of flames. Soon, it would engulf and swallow the bar. Although the smoke was thickening, the roaring sunset colors were vivid through the haze. The smoke would reach us and swallow us in a death embrace if we lingered. And if the building contained hazards that would accelerate the fire, releasing toxic chemicals...

Icy fear clutched at my insides.

We had to get out.

Sirens grew louder, indicating their approach. "'Bout time," I muttered. Okay, that wasn't fair. As a firefighter, I knew they hauled ass to get there as quick as possible. Being on the other end, waiting while each precious second ticked as the flames grew and the smoke intensified, cut my patience levels.

The firefighters arrived as we escaped the growing inferno and gulped for air. Since we worked a few towns away, we didn't recognize each other. Good. It wasn't time for small talk, especially in our choice of outfits.

"An explosion took out part of the back wall. The flames started there, but they're spreading toward the front. I think we have everyone off the main floor."

"Check the bathrooms," Maya said.

"And there might be some other rooms upstairs," I added.

"We got it," one said, and they ran into the club. Michel's club. Or what was left of it.

Michel. I ran around the back to find him. *If* he was still there.

I dashed to the back of the building where the wall had been blown out. Firefighters gathered onto the scene, but I didn't see Michel. On the ground, dark drops of what I presumed was blood sprinkled over the pavement. Swallowing the dread that rose, I searched for any more clues.

More drops. Although they appeared to spread randomly, by stepping back and taking a look at the bigger picture, I determined which way they led. I ran, following the blood trail down the block and around to a side street, and paused. The three of them were locked in battle, their fists pounding hard blows onto each other, resounding with a louder thud than expected. What the fuck were they made of? Concrete?

"Stop!" I screamed.

Michel looked over his shoulder at me, his eyes blazing

with a crimson hue. Blood dripped from his mouth. From fangs.

That couldn't be right. The only thing I knew had fangs were vampires. But vampires weren't real; they were a myth, a scary tale to explain mysterious occurrences. I didn't believe in the supernatural. Of course not, I was a rational woman. Most of the *mysterious* fires I'd come across in my line of work ended up being explained by a logical chain of events, often leading to an arsonist.

Maybe it was some weird goth guy fight club scenario. Glue fangs onto your teeth and fight. With a nervous laugh, I tried to convince myself. Yeah, that had to be it.

But what about the eyes? No contacts could give a person such a feral look. And the blood? That would take some calculated planning.

And the explosion?

My rational explanations flew away as sure as the debris that had floated through Michel's office after the wall blew out.

"Nike, get away from here," Michel said. "Now!"

The large man with long, dirty-blond, wavy hair let go of Michel and turned toward me.

"Nike, is it?" He sneered. "So, you're the one who has Michel all riled up? I wouldn't believe he'd have feelings for a human after all this time, if I didn't sense it myself."

The hair on the back of my neck rose like caterpillars sensing danger. The smaller, darker of the two men, or whatever they were, had turned to face me too. His monstrous eyes glared. His hungry, beastlike presence indicated he wasn't human. He didn't say anything. Could he even talk?

"Let's see what it is about this little human that had Michel all wound up." He took a sniff in the air. "Maybe it's her taste."

My taste? If the fire had triggered an instinct to run

earlier, this beast had flared it up to epic levels. All my senses fired with adrenaline, screaming *run!* I turned and bolted, sprinting from whatever those men were, who clearly posed a threat to me. Dark laughter and roars followed me, followed by a thud.

"Leave her!" Michel shouted. "Your quarrel is with me."

Despite the terror I felt, I turned back to see what happened. Michel had jumped on the blond one and they rolled on the ground. The short, dark one joined in.

I sprinted toward my VW, parked a few blocks away. The acrid smell of smoke and fire permeated the air around me. More fire trucks had arrived. I thought of Maya.

She's safe. She got out with you.

True. She was probably helping out, or giving a report as to what happened. I'd get in touch with her later.

When I reached my orange Beetle, I turned the ignition and slammed my stiletto boot down on the accelerator. Instincts screamed *drive!* but I couldn't leave Michel back there. Two on one was not right, in any situation. I was a firefighter and he needed help. I couldn't just drive away.

With a shake of my head, I turned around, heading to the monsters who'd threatened to taste me.

Only moments had passed, or was it minutes? My sense of time was off. Every second was pounding out with an intensity I'd never experienced.

I cried out with relief when I spotted Michel, still fighting both monsters.

"Michel," I yelled. "Get in."

It took him a moment to realize what was happening, but then he leaped so quickly from their grasps I wasn't sure how it happened. Within an instant, he was in the car beside me. How the fuck did he move so fast?

"Go!" he shouted.

I slammed my foot on the gas. Michel grabbed the

steering wheel and drove straight into them. The impact sounded like metal on concrete, not human flesh.

"Oh my God! Did we kill them?"

I glanced in the rearview mirror at the men, now lumps on the ground.

"Not that easy," he replied. "Let's get out of here before they recover."

Sure enough, they were getting back to their feet. Three gray figures ran to them and the fight resumed. Holy fuck. It couldn't be…

They resembled the gargoyle statues in the club. Stone statues—which now moved and fought. What I thought I'd seen with a flying gray shape during the fire must have been real after all and not a trick of the smoke.

"Michel, what the hell are those?"

"My guards. They'll deal with it. Now go!"

The front end of my car was damaged, but still drivable. I took control of the steering wheel and stepped on the gas pedal. When it lurched forward, I cried out with relief. I sped around the corner, not slowing down until we reached an on-ramp to the highway.

"Where should we go?"

"Not your place," he said. "It won't take long for them to figure out who you are and where you live."

"Oh God!"

"Get over to 95."

After I maneuvered onto a road that would lead me to the highway, I asked, "North or South?"

"North. We're going up to Maine."

"Maine? Why there?"

"I have a friend who has a place up there. It's secluded. We'll be safe."

As I drove, I took some more deep yoga breaths to try to refocus and calm down. How many times had I done that already tonight? First, reining in my feelings for Michel. Second, with a fire. And now, with this?

"I'm sorry about your car," he said. "I'll buy you a new one."

I jerked my head over to glance at him. So many questions burned in my brain, I didn't know where to start. For several minutes, we drove in silence. I focused on the drive while I sorted out my questions.

"The guards weren't human."

"No," he replied in a wary tone.

"What are they? And who were the guys who attacked?"

"One's an old friend."

"That didn't seem like a friendly encounter."

Michel didn't answer right away. "We had a falling out a long time ago."

"How long ago?"

"Quite some time."

"Why are you being evasive?"

He clenched his jaw. "It's better that you don't know."

My foot hovered over the brake pedal. I was ready to toss him on his ass. "Enough with the games. Tell me what the hell is going on, or I'll pull over and let you out here and we go our own ways."

Perhaps I was overreacting. Kicking someone out of the car on a highway wasn't something a rational person did. Yet not one aspect of the evening inspired me to act rational.

After he exhaled with an audible sigh, Michel said, "That is probably better for you." Then he rubbed his hand over his mouth. "No. They'd track your scent."

Track my scent? "What in holy hell are you talking about?"

"It's not apparent to humans, but to my kind…"

Michel may be strikingly hot and all, flaming my desires, but I didn't have time for evasiveness and word games.

"Listen, buddy, I just saw a wall blow up in the room I was in. A man who I'd just kissed sprouted fangs and jumped out of a second-story window. And now two men, *if* they even are considered men, are after me. Now you're telling me they can track my *scent.* So, cut the crap and be straight with me. Who the fuck are you? No, *what* are you? *Why* are they trying to kill you? And what the hell is going on?"

I took deep breaths to try to control my spiraling reaction.

Michel didn't answer right away. When I glanced in his direction, his expression was fierce. Conflicted.

"What I'm about to tell you isn't something I confide every day for good reason. Will you swear to keep this to yourself? For your own safety at the very least?"

Questions battled in my head, debating how I should respond. Curiosity won out. The cheeky bastard. "Yes."

All the tension that had emanated from us moments before vanished, replaced by a new ambiance that filled up the small space in my Beetle—anticipation. Specifically, mine.

"I was born outside of Paris in 1763," he said.

Damn it, was he messing with me? If so, this was bullshit. The look on his face appeared sincere, not that it meant anything.

"Did you just say the seventeen hundreds?"

"Yes. Please let me continue. I haven't told a human my story and I think it will be easiest if I tell it in one go. You can ask me questions after."

I blinked. Shit. Was he admitting that he wasn't human?

"Okay."

"Your history books tell you about the French Revolution, but they don't explain how it actually felt to live through that time. It was chaotic, thrilling, terrifying, and exhilarating. I have not experienced an era like that since."

Although questions swarmed my mind, I was unable to formulate any words and didn't want to interrupt the story.

"I served in a militia back then. One day our village was warned of an impending attack. I led my men to counter the charge. We fought the marauders most of the day. We lost many men, but we managed to fend off the attack and they retreated.

"I had left a small group at the gates to protect our village. They were overpowered by the attackers. They killed and raped. They burned many homes to the ground. My sister was killed. So was Ricard's wife. He blames me for her death and vowed revenge. That's why he wants to kill me."

He didn't continue, so I asked, "Why? You were attacked. How could you have prevented it?"

"He thinks we should have left more men back to protect the village."

"Do you think he's right?"

"That's a question I've been debating in my mind for two hundred years. I've been wracked with guilt and devastated by our losses. My sister. She was so young, so kind."

He spoke so softly when he spoke of his sister that I barely heard him. When I thought of how I'd feel if it had been my little brother, a wave of empathy swelled through me. Michel's guilt, his grief—how long had he shouldered it?

"What was her name?"

"Marguerite."

He shook his head as if shaking off a memory. "Overall I think it was the right decision. The battle was so close. If we had any fewer men, we might not have held them off."

"Did you explain that to Ricard?"

"Yes. He disagrees."

My head was swimming with all this information. "Wait. You were both human, right?"

"Yes."

"And now you're not?"

He answered, "No."

I shook my head as if trying to clear the cobwebs. "Why not?" We reached the interstate and I veered onto the ramp heading north.

"After the attack, we remained positioned at our camp before the village to fend off any additional advances. Ricard and I were on watch. One night a woman approached us. She had dark hair, pale skin, and wore a black flowing dress. We'd heard about a legend describing someone like her. A mysterious woman who haunted the battlefields, coming to men who were injured. Floating among them like a ghost, but acting in a much more sinister manner.

"I asked her who she was and what she wanted," Michel continued. "She didn't reply. A strange sensation filled me, like after drinking wine. It lulled me into a relaxed state. It was like she was captivating me to her will somehow. In a movement quicker than my eyes could process, she pounced upon me. She bit my neck and drank my blood. I tried to call out to Ricard, but couldn't. My voice wouldn't come out. I was trapped in my body, terrified, as she fastened her mouth upon my throat and continued to drink."

"Oh my God," I exclaimed, shooting a quick glance over at him. "What happened to you?"

"I'm not sure. Later, maybe days later, I awoke in the woods near our camp. And I was different, changed. Ricard wasn't there. An instinct rose in me, one I'd never felt before. It was a thirst for blood. So disturbing as my brain understood the vile compulsion, yet my body craved it with a hunger I couldn't stifle. An urge to return to camp filled me, to drink the blood of the men back there. To attack the very same men I had been tasked to protect! I was horrified. It took all my will to overcome that compulsion and redirect it. I attacked any animal that passed my way, biting them and drinking their blood. Anything to get rid myself of the thirst. I spent weeks that way, living in the woods and drinking the blood of animals. Occasionally when a human drifted into the woods alone and I was filled with thirst, I was unable to resist the urge."

My mouth had fallen open as I listened to his story. "Did you kill them?"

"I don't know. I hope not. After I fed, I felt so ashamed I ran off."

I shook my head to clear away the image. "And Ricard?" I asked.

"He must have been changed as well. I ran into him in the woods weeks later. He said, 'It's your fault they're dead.' I tried to explain it to him as I told you earlier. He attacked and we fought. No longer as two men, but two beasts. In the middle of the fight, we heard laughter. The dark-haired woman had reappeared.

"'How ridiculous', she said. 'I give you both the gift of immortality and the first thing you do is try to destroy each other.'

"'Who are you?' I asked. 'What have you done to us?'

"'My name isn't important. I'm a nightwalker. I thrive on blood. I'd seen you two in battle. The bravest of your lot. And I wanted your blood. When I drank, I sensed an infection in you,' she told me. 'An infected wound perhaps. You were dying. You just didn't know it yet. I gave you some of my blood and saved you from what was likely a horrid and painful death.'

"'Saved? Is that what you call this?' I replied. 'I've left my people and stalk animals in the woods!'

"'And me? Why did you change me?' Ricard asked.

"'I drank too much of your blood. I couldn't help myself. I could leave you there to die or change you. I decided you were too strong to let go and would be better off as one of us.'

"'Who's us?' I asked. 'There are others?'

"'Yes, of course. Nightwalkers are everywhere. But we usually live alone or in packs of two or three. We don't do well in groups.'

"She waved her hand. 'Enough talking. I'm separating you, like two little children.' She threw a ball of light at us and I felt a pull in my gut. I was thrown through the air and landed near some miles away.

"I spent the next twenty years learning self-control over my thirst, so I could inhabit society once again. I drank from stray animals in the street. Sometimes I slipped and attacked humans."

When I turned to look at him, he said, "It's been at least half a century. I've gotten better."

He flashed a smile that sent a ripple of excitement down through my core. Strange, considering he was talking about drinking blood.

"I moved to Paris and met others of my kind. They explained our nature and showed me how to live in the human world. They introduced me to an underground network where you could connect with humans who were willing to let you drink from them for the right price. With safety measures in place, so you didn't drink too much and kill them."

Wondering what types of safety measures could be implemented, I hadn't paid attention to the exits. Were we in New Hampshire yet? I scanned the signs; it looked like the tolls were ahead.

"I don't even know what to think about what you've just told me," I said. "If I hadn't seen what I saw tonight, I wouldn't believe you. But I did."

"It's not something to lie about."

"The guards—they looked like gargoyles."

"Right," he said.

"Are you shitting me?"

"No. In my situation, and with all the supernatural characters that come to Vamps, I need strong bodyguards. Gargoyles are the best there is. They watch from stone. And their strength is beyond that of a nightwalker."

Holy shit, this was insane. How could I be in a car driving with a vampire who had gargoyles for bodyguards? Someone who I'd lusted over for months admitted that he wasn't human. Not anymore, at least. My brain wrestled with information it never expected to process.

"I agree. I mean, I hope nobody would lie about something like that." I peered over at him. Damn, he was striking. But I had to think about driving away to a safe house, not admiring his brilliant features. "Can I just focus on driving for a bit while I try to process what you just told me?"

"Of course, *chérie*, I understand. Take all the time you need."

"I'm going to put some music on." Music was always the surest way to calm me.

"Want me to put something on for you?"

"Sure. Can you plug in my phone?"

After he connected the phone, the car was filled with Fiona Apple appealing to her lover while singing *On the Bound*. Oh, how I loved this song. But something about the intense feelings a woman sang to her lover made me shift with discomfort with Michel so close.

My phone shuffled through songs that weren't so intense about passionate love, relieving the underlying tension. We listened to music as we drove up to the New Hampshire border.

Michel's story played again in my head as I tried to make

sense of it. I hadn't noticed we had passed over the bridge into Maine until Michel interrupted. "Take the next exit."

"Okay." I moved into the right lane to exit. "Where are we going?"

"Stay on this road for a while."

I slowed down to the speed limit, which I often found difficult after driving on the highway for a while. We drove in silence for several more minutes.

"How did you end up here?" I asked.

"In New England?"

"Yes."

"I traveled around the world. The tranquility of a New England coastal town appealed to me."

"And donors?"

"Salem is full of them."

"Isn't it called the Witch City?"

"All kinds of characters are attracted to Salem. Supernatural elements everywhere."

Other parts of his story came back to me.

"What about the other uh, *thing*, with Ricard?" I asked, not sure what to call the freaky little beast that tried to attack us.

"I don't know. They must have met up at some point after we parted ways. Or maybe Ricard changed him."

After several minutes, Michel said, "Turn left at that unmarked road ahead."

The farther we drove, the more widely spaced the houses became. Eventually, the street lights disappeared where it was sparsely populated and I put on my high beams.

"Is this the first time you've run into Ricard since seeing the woman who changed you?"

"No."

I waited for an explanation. When none came, I prodded. "And?"

"He's been tracking me down for years. London, Budapest, Barcelona, Montreal."

"What happens? Do you fight?"

"Not usually. I slip away when I see an opportunity."

"Is he trying to kill you?"

"Yes."

"Does he want to kill me, too?"

He hesitated. "Most likely. To get back at me."

"Why don't you fight him? End it for once?"

His face contorted into a tormented look. "He was my friend. My brother. He thinks he's avenging the death of his wife."

How someone sympathized for that monster perplexed me. "Michel, it's been over two hundred years. Enough for several human lifetimes. He needs to let go of his anger and you need to let go of the guilt."

"Those are human emotions. We aren't human any longer. Can I ask you something now?"

"Sure."

"What happened at Vamps?"

The images from the fire came back to me. What a shitty night.

Taking a deep breath and exhaling, I summarized the events into an abridged version.

"After you jumped out the building, I went downstairs. Fire from the blast quickly spread through the club."

I noticed him bristle once again.

"What is it?"

"Fire."

"What about it?"

"I don't like it."

"Oh. A vampire thing?"

He didn't answer. "And you're okay?" Out of the corner of my eye, I saw him scanning my body.

"Looking for wounds?" I asked. "Don't worry. I'm fine."

"How about the others? Did anyone get hurt?"

"My friend Maya and I think everyone got out safely."

"Good," he said, placing a finger on his chin and staring straight ahead, deep in thought.

I should try to reach Maya. Although I didn't like to talk while I drove, it had been a crazy night and I had to check in with her. When I called her, it went into voice mail. I left a message to let her know I was okay and would call in the morning.

After a few more minutes, he said, "Pull into the driveway on the right."

I took the right and followed a dirt driveway down away from the road. It led to a tiny Tudor facing the Atlantic.

"We're here."

"Where are we?" I asked.

"You'll see."

Michel held my hand as he led me up a stone walkway to an old cottage. I hesitated on the doorstep.

"I won't hurt you," he said. "I promise."

CHAPTER 4

I gazed into those bright-blue eyes. Eyes that weren't human. Was that why they were so entrancing? And could I trust him? *Should* I trust him?

"Please, Nike. Come in. All I want to do right now is protect you from harm. Not be the cause of it."

He looked sincere and I wanted to believe him. Did he care about me? Or was he just luring me in?

"I'm a fool to go into a house with someone who admitted a thirst for human blood," I said. "But I suppose I don't stand much more chance out here either."

"I confided in you. That's not something I would do unless I had feelings for you."

The cynical part inside of me said *it's easy to confess when you know you'll silence the listener.* But a much bigger part of me wanted nothing more than to be alone with him in this cottage.

He opened the door to a welcoming living room with a basket of afghans next to a sofa and another one in between two Victorian chairs. Equipped for a cool night on the New England coast.

"I'd light a fire to keep you warm, but under the circumstances…" His voice trailed off.

I forced a smile. "Enough fire for one night." And I nodded in his direction. "And you're clearly not a fan. Can it harm, you know—people, um, those like you?"

Michel smiled, but didn't answer. "How about a hot cocoa?"

I didn't blame him. If fire could harm him, why would he tell me, a human, how to hurt him? "That would be great. Thanks."

After I peeled off the stiletto boots of my sore feet, I exhaled. They looked great, but constricted my feet. Then I curled up under an afghan on the sofa as best I could manage in the tight dress.

Michel grabbed a mug and a package of some gourmet hot cocoa. I had admired his broad back and shoulders at the gym many times when I thought he wasn't looking. Now I watched him unabashedly as he filled the kettle, my mind reeling with the tale he had just told. We were here together in a secluded house overlooking the ocean. How much had changed in only a few hours.

When he handed me the steaming mug, I asked, "What do we do now?"

Michel took a moment to answer. "Stay here," he said. "And get to know each other better."

I swallowed as he sat down next to me.

"Don't be afraid of me. I would never hurt you."

The worries about being with a nightwalker rose to the surface. "How can I be sure? You're not even human."

"I was once. And tonight I felt more human than I had in a hundred years."

"When? Why?"

"When I was with you upstairs. When I thought something would happen to you. I haven't felt emotions like that in a long time."

I took a sip of the hot cocoa to try to control my racing heartbeat. Michel ran a finger softly across my cheek and lower lip, making me tremble slightly. I looked into his eyes, only inches away from mine. Those eyes that always captivated me. Was it all just part of his charm? My breath quickened.

No, I had to focus. Think about my safety and not my libido. Too many thoughts were racing through my head.

"You don't even know me," I said. "Why would you care?"

Michel leaned back. "Good question. I wonder that myself. I might not be able to explain what I feel, but there is no doubt my feelings are real."

Breathe. Just breathe.

"I'm making you nervous," he said. "I apologize. What will make you more comfortable?"

I shifted. "Well, getting to know more about you might be a start. I mean, what you told me in the car about centuries ago, that's mind-blowing. Maybe we should talk about more recent things."

"What would you like to know?"

Where to start? I waved my hand in the air. "Tell me about the club. And the gym. And whatever other businesses you own."

"All right. Once I got past the brooding phase of immortality, I sought new experiences. What was the point of not dying if you didn't find a way to live?"

That was an interesting way to put it.

"I settled here, around forty years ago, and began to invest in real estate. Many commercial properties eventually became quite profitable. Then it was time to invest in some fun projects. I own restaurants, but they provide little pleasure since I don't eat like a human any longer. I tried rock climbing one night at a gym near Boston and liked it. So, I built one here in Cat's Cove."

"For fun?" Imagine that—having enough money that creating a gym was considered a pastime.

He nodded. "Oui."

"And Vamps?"

"I had an empty warehouse that I wanted to fill. I thought I'd try for something here in this quiet community, an experiment at first. I'd visited clubs around the world. The ones that intrigued me most were ones with a darker edge, inviting to those who didn't quite fit elsewhere. Why not create one there?"

"It seemed to have turned out well."

He smiled. "It attracts quite a crowd."

Did he mean people? Or others like him? "More vampires? Gargoyles? What else?"

"I prefer nightwalkers," he said.

"So…yes?"

"Not often…but yes, some nightwalkers come, too. Gargoyles are a type of shapeshifter. We've had several pass through."

"I'm almost afraid to ask this, but what are shapeshifters?"

"Shifters are able to shift from human form to another, such as stone gargoyles, but also lion shifters, wolf shifters, tiger shifters—you get the picture."

I did? No, I needed a zillion years to come to grips with what I was hearing.

Holy shit. My world turned stranger by the minute. How many vampires—err, nightwalkers—and shapeshifters had I encountered in the past?

"I need some air."

I walked to the back door and opened it to a breathtaking view of the ocean. The winds had kicked up, causing the waves to battle against the rocks below. I tried to concentrate, to focus on rational thought.

I peeled off the thigh-high stockings that had made my legs look sexy as hell in those stiletto boots, yet now were torn so badly I looked like an utter mess. I walked barefoot on the sand on the beach away from the house. The stupid dress was constricting, which made it difficult to pick up the pace.

Think clearly.

It was insane to think about getting involved with someone who wasn't even human. Yes, I knew this. I was a practical girl, not a romantic one. Relationships were difficult as it was. If it was Maya in this situation, I'd tell her she was acting like a stupid, lovesick teenager.

That would be after I didn't believe whatever nonsense she was spewing about supernatural creatures. I'd tell her they don't exist. Hell, I wouldn't believe such beings existed until I encountered three of them tonight, two of whom were trying to kill me.

I was being hunted. After the adrenaline of the fire and escape from those monsters faded that truth settled on me like a black veil. Why? Because I'd been with Michel tonight. *The first time I've been alone with him.* Insane. My timing couldn't be worse.

Maybe if I got away from him, I'd be safe. After all, their issue was with him, not me. I quickened my pace to break into run. Running away from him. Running to safety.

I'd left my phone inside the cottage. As soon as I found one, I'd call Maya. She'd find a way to get to me and we'd figure out what to do next. Although it was the middle of the night, she'd be there for me.

An unsettling sensation crawled over my skin. I turned to look behind me. Nobody was following me. I pushed myself into a full-blown sprint.

Don't look back.

Michel

I hated waiting. Hiding in this safe house made it seem like we were waiting for something to happen.

I paced in front of the fireplace. Why did Ricard have to come tonight of all nights? Fate was clearly a twisted force with a warped sense of humor.

I almost had Nike. I finally broke through the closed off veneer she enclosed herself in before everything went to hell. The look of passion that burned in her eyes earlier when we were upstairs had been replaced by a different one, as if debating with herself in her head. If things had developed between us, I would have told her about myself, eventually. It was hardly something to reveal on the first date. It wasn't even that, technically. Our first intimate *encounter*. Figures Ricard had to screw everything up. He had a gift of irking me at the worst moments.

I grabbed a trinket from the side table and crushed it in my hand and then watched as the ceramic pieces fell through my fingers. How easily it was destroyed. I barely even thought about it. Fragile. Almost as fragile as a human.

Like Nike.

Being with me was dangerous for her. Although we had only connected a short while ago, an urge to protect her grew in me. I couldn't explain it. It had started that one and only time when I'd belayed her in the rock climbing gym a month ago. The trust she had to place in me instilled something I hadn't felt for anyone in a long time. There had been women in my past. And I'd belayed countless climbers in the gym. But this connection with Nike was inexplicable. And overpowering.

I would kill anyone who tried to hurt her.

If I cared about her, I should let her go, send her some

place safe. Ricard would hunt us down eventually. We could only hide for so long.

I broke the larger ceramic pieces into a pile of dust. How tragic it was to have to let her go so soon. We had just had our first kiss. Our first and last.

But I had to let her go.

Nike

My lungs started to burn from the quickened pace and the sharp cool air of the ocean. I slowed to a walk again.

What was I doing? Where the hell was I running to? It wouldn't keep me safe. Michel had mentioned how those fuckers would track my scent. My *scent!* I took a deep breath so as not to let that terrifying concept make me continue to act irrationally.

I could run and bemoan the circumstance I'd landed myself in, or I could move on. But I wasn't a person who dwelled. I dealt with the situation. It was more practical. Why waste time rehashing what couldn't be changed? So, some shit had happened tonight. Time to assess the situation from another angle than fear, which might lead me to make a fatal mistake.

The man I'd wanted for so long was waiting inside for me. He was trying to protect me. And what was I doing? Running off on my own to escape creatures I wouldn't have a chance of taking on.

Plus, with my infatuation with Michel that had grown over the months, the scenario of ending up in a cabin alone with him was far more exhilarating and fantastic than any fantasy I'd concocted on my own. I'd be a fool to run away.

I pictured Maya raising an eyebrow and saying, "What are you, nuts? Get back in there and stop being so bloody stubborn!"

Time to toughen up and go after what I wanted. Which, if my dreams were any indication, was Michel.

I breathed in the saltwater air. Life was short. It could've ended for me tonight if Michel hadn't intervened.

Then again, I wouldn't have been in danger if I wasn't with him. But it was too late now to debate the cause and effect. What happened had happened. They would kill me to exact revenge. I was better off with Michel. Whatever we had to face, we were better off doing so together.

Plus, it was where every fiber in my being yearned to redirect me. Back to him.

Enough! I don't want to think anymore.

Taking a deep breath, I turned back toward the house, ready to face whatever fate had in store with me. With Michel.

Michel

I played with the remains of the ceramic pieces on the end table, brooding over how I would lose her all too soon. The sound of the French door opening distracted me. When she entered, I forgot my inner torment and stood. She was back.

"Ça va?" I said, slipping into my native language. "Are you all right?"

"Yes," she said almost breathlessly, walking toward me with a vigorous stride.

Within moments, she was before me. She put her hand behind my head and pushed up to her tiptoes, leaning forward. She paused for a second, looking into my eyes, and then at my lips.

She kissed me. Slowly at first, as if exploring and savoring me. And then she pressed her lips against mine more urgently, with a slow-releasing passion.

I responded instantly to the touch of those soft, full lips.

Whatever torment I had over having to lose her disappeared at that moment. How could I think rationally when this stunning creature kissed me?

I wrapped my arms around her lower back and arched down to meet her lips more fully.

She pulled away briefly. "I've wanted you for so long."

Her pupils darkened to a seductive, smoky green under her lowered eyelids. The passion in them heightened my own. I savored her lips and neck as I moved her toward the bedroom. Pushing open the partially ajar door, I led her to the canopied bed.

Laying her gently on her back, I leaned over her, put my hands on her cheeks and looked into her eyes. "Nike, I've been intrigued by you, but kept away for your sake. But tonight—tonight I couldn't help myself. You were too close. You smelled so good. God help me, but I want you."

"Yes. Please, now."

Reluctant to leave those soft, pouty lips but eager to explore the rest of her, I kissed down the side of her slender neck. Her scent and the throbbing of her pulse under my lips were almost too much. My fangs emerged and I salivated, the promise of a delectable meal dangling before me. I fought the urge to taste her blood right then, despite the almost over-powering temptation.

When she moaned a low, soft sigh, it pushed me close to the edge. My fangs hovered over her veins and the desire for her blood rushed through me. Scraping teeth over her skin, all I had to do was pierce her skin and I would taste that sweet nectar, let it run down my throat, enflame all my senses...

No! I had to regain control. I closed my eyes and forced myself to ignore the calling to taste her. Once again, I was flooded with a different desire—the desperate need to bury myself deep within her.

I kissed her skin down from her enticing neck to the top of her breasts pushing up out of the black leather corset. Kissing her softly and gently licking her skin, I grew more excited as she writhed beneath my kisses.

When I pulled the strings of her corset loose, her breasts spilled out, as if relieved to be free of the constraints. They were beautiful, the perfect size to hold and taste. A jolt of excitement shot down to my cock. I grasped a pink nipple in my mouth and sucked gently, barely scraping my teeth along its sensitive peak.

"Oh God, that feels good," she murmured.

I kissed a path down her torso and around her navel. She breathed more rapidly as I eased the leather dress down around her hips and slid it off her.

Seeing her with only the tiniest of black lace panties on made me inhale sharply.

"*Mon Dieu.* You are utterly beautiful."

Leaning down, I continued soft kisses past her navel. I ran a finger along the top seam of her lace panties and she squirmed beneath me. Inching a finger slowly inside the brocade lace string, I tugged it down.

"Yesss," she hissed.

I pulled the panties down her legs and off her feet, tossing them aside. Seeing her fully naked filled me with an animalistic craving. Her scent filled me with sensual urges as well as one to bite her. I was all too aware of her blood pulsing hypnotically under her smooth, pale skin. I had to refocus on the other overwhelming desire I had, which was to get inside her.

Oh, to do both would be... I almost couldn't think of the sweet ecstasy.

"Are you okay?" she asked.

"Just regaining control," I said through a clenched jaw.

"*Très belle.* I want to take you right now. But I also want to slow time, so I can savor every inch of you."

"Don't wait too long," she said. "I want you now. Right now."

Nike rose and kissed me fervently, pulling me down on top of her. She tugged at my T-shirt, yanking it over my head. When she paused to stare at my chest, the dark sparkle in her widening eyes filled me with pride. I resisted the urge to pump my chest out more. She ran a finger down the center of my chest. Her touch, so soft and light dancing down toward my abs, made me tremble.

When she kissed my shoulder and gently bit it, I moaned. She moved her hands across my chest, following it with her soft lips, going down, down to the top of my jeans.

"You don't know what you're doing to me."

When she touched my cock, I thought I'd lose control. She ran her hand down over it with a feather-light stroke that drove me near mad. Then reaching for my buckle, she unfastened it and pulled down the zipper. My cock stiffened even more knowing her fingers were just inches away.

"Impressive," she said as she tugged my pants down around my hips.

I pulled them the rest of the way down, quickly took off my shoes and socks until all that was left were my black boxer-briefs.

"Are you sure you want this?" I asked.

"Yes. Oh yes." She tugged down my underwear. Her jaw dropped open. "Wow."

She looked me straight in the eye. That draw to her rose. I wanted this woman more than anyone I could remember. Being so close to her was as intoxicating and addicting as the taste of blood. I wanted her so desperately, I could taste her scent.

I kissed her again and pulled her close Her fingers moved

along my thighs as she inched closer up my leg. When her fingers grazed my cock, I moaned. She rubbed me gently and I pressed myself toward her, grabbing for her perfect ass.

Pressing my cock against her, I reveled in the sensation of her against my flesh.

"Oh God, yes," she moaned. "I'm ready. Please, just do it."

"*Oui, ma belle.*"

"Wait—do you have protection? You know, a condom?"

Resisting a smirk for that awful human necessity, I explained, "I can't get you pregnant and I don't carry human diseases. But if you want me to wear one, I will."

She bit her lip. "I'm not used to this." She relaxed and pulled me close. "Forget that. Don't make me wait any longer."

Not needing any more encouragement, I penetrated her warm flesh slowly. She pushed against me at first and then relaxed as I entered more deeply.

All sorts of visions filled my mind, competing with emotions I hadn't felt, well—maybe ever. When had I made love to someone that I'd already felt such a strong connection to somehow? I couldn't remember. Although there were many women over the centuries, she held a special place in my psyche. I didn't understand, yet knew I'd do anything to protect her.

She closed her eyes and bit her lower lip. I penetrated her slowly at first, but then with each subsequent movement, I went deeper inside her.

"Oh yes," she said.

I pumped into her harder and she cried out.

"Do you like that? Want more?" I asked.

"Yes," she hissed.

I fucked her harder, watching as she turned her head to the side on the pillow and bit her lip. Then she reached up around my back, pulling herself up toward me. I groaned as I felt her muscles contract tighter against my cock.

I fought to focus as she dug her nails into my back. "Yes, Michel. Just like this."

I kept up the pace as she frantically grabbed my back and arms and pulled herself up closer. Her breathing escalated and she let out a soft moan.

Then she pulled me tighter. "Oh my God!"

Her pussy tightened and began to pulse. Her juices flowed over me, slickening us both. The scent of her was intoxicating and I had to fight the urge to bite her.

"*Oui*, Nike."

She let her head roll back toward the pillow and moaned softly. I slowed down the tempo, letting her recover from her orgasm. When she opened her eyes again, I resumed pumping her hard.

She squealed and reached for my ass. The touch of her hands there excited me greatly and I pumped her with deep hard thrusts. Deep within me, a powerful surge blinded me as it rushed to my cock. After a few more pounding thrusts, I released inside her, dropping my head back as I growled.

"Nike." I settled my body on top of hers, careful not to crush her, and she wrapped her arms around me. Her heart beat against my chest.

After a few moments, I rolled onto my side and wrapped my arms around her. I couldn't speak while we cooled off. After a few minutes, I said, "You were magnificent. Everything all right?"

She flashed me a flirtatious smile. "How could it not be after that?" Her lips turned downward and a furrow mark appeared between her brows. "But, I can't help but think about things."

"About what?"

She shook her head. "Now isn't the time. I have too many questions and no brain power left to formulate them."

"I'll answer them all when you're ready. Now why don't you get some rest? It's been a long day."

"And an even longer night," she said. "But can you sleep here? Or do you have to find a coffin or something?"

I chuckled. "I can sleep here with you. There are special light-blocking shades in here."

"You can't go out in the sun? That's not just a myth?"

"Unfortunately, not. But as long as I'm in a room that blocks the sunlight, I can stay awake during the day."

"The gym?"

"Yes. Have you ever noticed there are no windows in the climbing area?"

"No, I didn't. But now that you mention it, yes, you're right."

"I have a room so I can sleep there if I want to see clients during the day."

Her eyes showed her exhaustion. I needed to let her rest.

"You're tired. It's been a long night. The sun will be up soon." I brushed some hair away from her forehead and then kissed it. "Get some sleep, *ma belle*."

She repositioned herself on her side while I wrapped my arms around her and then we drifted off to sleep.

CHAPTER 5

N*ike*

When I awoke the next morning, I replayed what seemed like the most vivid nightmare and extremely erotic dream all wrapped into one. It all seemed so real—the fire, the men who attacked and…Michel.

Michel.

I ran a finger across my bottom lip, reliving the hot moments I had just dreamed about. None of my fantasies in the past had ever been so vivid, yet so complex.

I stretched out my legs and became aware of a body next to me. When I opened my eyes, the familiar outlines of a bedroom came through, where I'd dreamed I'd made love to Michel. The windows were covered with heavy curtains keeping out the sunlight.

It wasn't a dream; it was real. All of it.

When I rolled over and found Michel next to me, I sucked in my breath. He was handsome from afar with those intense blue eyes and strong physique. But, with him lying inches away, I appreciated the finer details about him, like his dark eyelashes and the highlights in his shoulder-length hair.

Fortunately, his eyes were closed, as I always felt a little giddy whenever I met his penetrating stare.

I admired the chiseled lips that often curled up in a joker-like smile. Details about him that would never change. He would remain forever young. Not wishing to wake him, I resisted the urge to reach out and touch those lips. I reveled in this moment where I could look at him. In the gym, I could only catch a glimpse here and there. Whenever he caught my eye or said hi, I'd quickly return the greeting and turn away in fear he could see my most intimate thoughts.

And last night, many of those thoughts became reality. I wanted to jump out of bed and squeal like a little girl. Maybe call Maya and tell her about the fantastic turn of events.

Maya.

The fire. The destruction. All that came back to me as well. Was everyone all right? I had to call Maya and find out what happened.

I sat up to look around the bedroom for a phone.

"Not going somewhere, I hope."

When I heard his deep voice, parts of my body reawakened, remembering his touch.

"I was just going to call Maya and see what happened."

"Yes, good idea. I hope you're not too long." He traced a finger down the side of my torso, which sent shivers through me.

Reluctant to leave, I said, "I'll be right back."

I stepped out the back door. When Maya didn't answer on the first five rings, my heart rate escalated.

"Hel-lo," said a groggy voice.

"Maya! It's me. Are you okay?"

"Nike? Yeah, I'm okay," she said. "You?"

"Fine. What happened after I left?"

"A whole load of emergency responders showed up. You know how it goes."

"Everyone okay?"

"Some people went to the hospital for observation, but I think they're going to be okay. Luckily, nobody was killed last night. That could have gone downhill fast. What a freakin' nightmare."

Especially for firefighters without their equipment. I exhaled. "I know."

"Hey, where are you? Last time I saw you, you ran off to find that hot guy you were having palpitations about. What was his name? Something French, right?"

"Michel. Um, yeah. Well, I found him."

"And?"

"I'm with him now."

"Holy shit, Nike! Get out!"

"Listen, it's a long story. I'll tell you later. But I just wanted to make sure everyone's okay."

"Don't make me wait. What the hell? We deal with a fire at Vamps and then you end up with that guy? Hot damn, we have a shit load to talk about. Let's grab some brunch later. Most of all, I want to hear all the nasty details!"

"Ha, ha. You wish. No, I can't meet up with you today. It's kind of complicated, but I'm not sure when I'll be back."

"What do you mean?" Maya said, a note of wariness in her tone. "Where are you? And why aren't you coming back?"

"Things are a little strange right now. I don't really understand it myself."

"What the hell, Nike? You're being weird."

"I'm fine. Just wanted to check in."

"I don't know what you're talking about, but don't do anything stupid. Be careful. And call me if something goes wrong. If this guy turns out to be some whack job and locks you in his basement, I will cut off his dick."

Maya's threat made me laugh despite the not so laughable

situation I'd landed myself into. "It's nothing like that. I'll call you soon."

After I hung up with Maya, I thought of other calls to make. Crap, I was on the schedule to work tomorrow. How should I explain my indefinite absence?

"Hey, it's me, Nike," I said to the firefighter who answered. "Is the captain in?"

"Not today. What's up?"

"Can you let him know I won't be in for the next few days?"

"You sick?"

"No. I have some urgent personal matters to attend to out of town. I had to leave right away."

"Is everything okay?"

"Yes, it will be. Just make sure you let him know and I'll get in touch as soon as I can." The last person I wanted to field questions from right now was my boss.

"Will do," he said. "Hey, did you hear about the nightclub fire in Cat's Cove last night?"

That was a subject I didn't want to get into, so I made some excuse saying I had to go.

"Everything okay?" Michel asked when I hung up the phone.

"Yes. Some people were hospitalized for observation, but they should be okay."

"I made some calls as well. A lot of damage at the club, but that can be fixed. My priority right now is keeping us safe."

His words reminded me of the danger we were in, being hunted by some creatures when I didn't exactly know what they were or what they were capable of. "What about your guards? The—uh—gargoyles?" It sounded bizarre to utter that sentence.

"They are on watch. Looking for Ricard and the other nightwalker."

The image of gargoyles hunting nightwalkers seemed better suited for a comic book than my reality. "I'm going to take a quick shower and clean up."

"And maybe come back to bed after?" he suggested with a naughty grin.

"We'll see," I said, turning my head over my shoulder with a flirty smile. How did he snap me from being worried about my safety to thinking about more primal desires?

Although there was nothing I'd rather do at the moment than hop back into bed with Michel for a torrid morning, I needed to clear my head. Too much had happened since last night and I still didn't know if I'd processed any of it.

I turned the water up as hot as I could stand and stayed there trying to make sense of it all.

First, I had spent the night with the man I'd wanted for months. It was even more spectacular than what I had ever imagined.

Second, he wasn't human. How or when I would process that fact would probably be a while.

Third, two creatures tried to kill us last night and managed to hurt many people in the process. Since they chose last night—the night I finally had my moment with Michel—to attack, now they were after me as well.

That was a lot of shit to deal with. If Michel were any other guy, I'd probably run far away and try to put it all behind me. But, I'd already debated enough on that matter and had chosen to stay.

I found some fruity shampoo and vanilla body wash to clean up the mess from last night. When the dirt washed off, I noticed a few nasty scrapes on my legs and arms. Great, so my first night with Michel I must have really looked like a dirty ho, literally covered in dirt. Luckily, it was dark.

After rinsing off, I wrapped myself in a white fluffy towel and walked back into the bedroom.

"You look ravishing," he said.

"Without any of my toiletries or makeup—I'm afraid to look."

Michel climbed out of bed. "Even more beautiful than last night. And I thought you looked amazing then."

He maneuvered my shoulders to point me toward the mirror. "Look at yourself. Stunning."

I looked in the mirror and saw me standing there clad only in a towel with wet hair hanging down to my shoulders. That, and the hottest guy I had ever seen standing behind me.

Wait, not a guy, really.

"I can see you," I said.

He looked at me oddly. "I see you too."

"No, in the mirror, I mean. You cast a reflection."

When he laughed, I didn't see any signs of his fangs.

"And your fangs. Where are they?"

"Don't worry about all that now. We have plenty of time to separate fact from myth, or understand my physiology."

Michel ran one hand along my right side, light enough that I could barely feel his touch through the fabric.

"Right now, I want to explore your physiology."

He bent down and kissed my neck. My body instantly responded; my neck tilted to the side to allow him greater access and a tingling stirred between my legs.

"*Si belle,*" he whispered.

As I watched him in the mirror, I grew more excited. Not only from watching him kiss me, but also seeing a lustful look appear on my face. I'd never seen myself like that before, never had sex in front of a mirror or on video. I had to admit, it was turning me on.

"Do you want a little help toweling off?" Michel asked between kisses.

"Yes," I murmured.

Michel unwrapped the towel from my body and I stood there, vulnerable next to him in his black pants.

"I'm naked," I said, turning away.

"You have an incredible body," he said. "Look at yourself."

I took another look in the mirror. Part of me wanted to cover myself up with the towel again. But as I watched Michel kiss my neck, toward my shoulder, a bigger part of me wanted to watch and wait. And have more of this.

He ran his hand over my stomach and up to a breast, fondling it gently. Then he lightly scraped his teeth over my shoulder and I closed my eyes, reveling in the sensation.

When his breath warmed one of my breasts, my nipples immediately tightened into hardened points.

When I reopened my eyes, he stared at me as he teased my nipple with his tongue. Lightly licking it and then gently sucking it. Looking in the mirror, it was a strange, erotic sensation to watch it from a different angle.

He spent some time on my other breast, alternating between teasing and sucking. It was almost too much to take.

Then he kissed down my midriff, first down the center around my bellybutton, and then along each side. My flesh tingled under his lips as I anticipated his next move and wanted more.

"Open your legs. Let me look at you."

I felt self-conscious at first, but I obeyed, feeling more vulnerable than ever.

And then I felt his warm breath as he kneeled just inches from my sex. My pulse quickened and I closed my eyes.

"I want you to watch."

I reopened my eyes. He leaned forward and lightly kissed me. My eyes drifted closed immediately as I sank into the pleasure.

A moment later, I remembered he wanted me to watch.

LISA CARLISLE

Sure enough, his intense gaze was fixed on my face in the mirror as he teased me with his fingers.

"Michel," I whispered.

He spread my folds and inserted a finger, pulling it in and out slowly. Then he licked me up one side and down the other. I moaned in pleasure.

He continued to move his tongue around, licking all of me, except my sensitive nub. My hips rose and with it, my desire for more.

He worked me with his tongue and fingers, teasing me and driving me insane. I watched us in the mirror, captivated. My breath came out rough pants.

Finally, his tongue was on my clit and I cried out in relief. I'd never been so desperate for anyone before. He shifted focus, increasing the pressure there with his skilled tongue, and I thought I'd go mad. It felt so good.

As he quickened the pace, I ran my fingers through his hair. "Yes. Don't stop."

He increased the pressure and my pants turned into soft cries. "Oh yeah. Right there."

And then a buildup inside me grew so strong that my body stiffened, from my thighs all the way down to my toes. Watching us in the mirror heightened the experience to a new level. I came with such a powerful quake I thought my legs might collapse.

Michel steadied me and then pulled himself up.

I didn't think I could find words. When my brain finally caught up, I said, "That was incredible."

"We're just getting started."

He stepped behind me and cupped one of my breasts. He pulled off his pants and I watched him in the mirror as he grasped his cock. He bent down slightly as he moved the head between my folds. Then he inserted the tip into my channel, which still faintly pulsed from my orgasm.

He pushed it in an inch or so a couple of times, and then a little more, and then finally, he pushed his cock deep within me, making me moan.

He moved both hands down to my waist and I bent forward. I watched in the mirror as he pumped me from behind, grabbing my shoulders. Heat rolled through my core as I watched him fuck me. It was so raw. And so exciting to see his face intense with passion as he drove in.

My entire body glowed with a fiery, pulsing heat, as I tipped closer and closer…

"Oh my God. Michel. Oh God."

I pressed my hands against the mirror as I braced myself for more.

"Ah, Nike," he murmured.

And then he drove me over the edge.

I didn't leave the bedroom until the afternoon. Already my internal clock felt screwy. Luckily, I was used to it, after years of long shifts as a firefighter. Michel went back to sleep since this was his normal sleeping hours, but I had too much on my mind.

I found a loose pair of pants and a sweater that would do for now, but unfortunately had to put on the stiletto boots. Pulling the pants down over them so they wouldn't be as conspicuous, I checked my appearance in a mirror to see if I looked presentable. I couldn't help but grin, thinking of the last time I had looked in a mirror.

Then I left a note with my phone number and slipped out the cottage to drive around town and look for some shops. If we were going to be here for a few days, I needed clothes and toiletries. And food. Most definitely.

Did Michel eat food? He mentioned restaurants provided little enjoyment, yet he had drunk with me last night. Or maybe that was just a ploy to look human. Just in case, I better get enough for two.

I retraced the route we had come down last night until I reached a main drag. Then I grabbed my phone to pull up a map to see what was nearby.

Phone was dead. Figured. Now I needed a charger too.

Two hours later, I returned to the cottage with some staples.

When I entered the cottage, the drapes were still drawn shut. Michel was sitting on the sofa with a reading lamp on nearby.

"*Tu vas bien?*" he asked, standing up. "Are you all right? Where were you?"

"I'm fine," I said, putting my bags down and peeling off the boots. "I didn't want to disturb you and I needed to get a few things."

"I tried calling and you didn't answer."

"My phone died. I got a charger. Sorry, I didn't know what kind of charger you would need."

"That's okay, I used the house phone. I apologize if I sound like a jealous boyfriend. But I was worried, considering the circumstances of last night..." His voice trailed off.

Seeing the concern on his face and realizing it was for my well-being almost stopped me in my tracks. Did he actually care for me? Me, just a human? Nothing really to his kind, except a food source.

A part of me almost laughed. If any other guy questioned me about my whereabouts as he just had, I would've rolled my eyes. Then I'd tell them to back off and stop invading my privacy.

What did I do in this situation? About as opposite a reaction as I could think of. I walked over to him, looked up into those eyes and said, "Don't worry. I'm fine. I'm here. With you."

He pulled me into a hug and I buried my face into his broad chest, relishing the sense of warmth and safety in his protective embrace.

"With me," he said. After a moment, he said, "I know too little about you, Nike. If something happened to you, I wouldn't even know who to contact. Do you have family here?"

I pulled my face away with reluctance. "Not too far. They live in Rhode Island."

"Tell me about them." He glanced down at me. "Tell me about you."

Talking about myself was one of my least favorite topics, but since I'd grilled him on his past, I couldn't play coy. "It's just my dad and two brothers, one older and one younger. My dad and brother are cops. My youngest brother is in the Army."

"Your mother?"

I swallowed a lump. "She died when I was eight. Cancer."

"I'm sorry, *ma belle*."

I took a fortifying breath. "It was a long time ago."

"What made you become a firefighter and not a cop?"

I smiled, turning away. "You'll laugh."

"I won't," he replied in earnest.

"A movie. A bad one at that. I love B-movies and there was one I watched when I was thirteen that had a fire. For some reason, I got fixated on the firefighters responding to the fire, helping people. I decided it was what I wanted to do."

When I faced him again, Michel grinned.

"You said you wouldn't laugh," I raised my index finger.

"I'm not," he protested. "It's a smile. I think it's a good story." He furrowed a brow. "Hold on. I'll be right back."

He returned a few minutes later with an ancient appearing VHS player and a box of tapes. "Maybe you'll find some bad movies in here."

My eyes widened. "I hope so." I fingered through the dusty VHS tapes. Mostly John Hughes movies, but one I lifted in triumph—The Rocky Horror Picture Show. "So good."

Michel laughed. "We'll watch it tonight. I have to make a few calls first."

While Michel checked in with his employees, I brewed tea with some spices I found in the kitchen cabinets. I took it out onto the deck to give him some privacy.

The sun was setting over the sea and I thought the color of the sun reflected on the waves reminded me of the colors that danced in a fire. I wanted to tell Michel to come out, but stopped myself. This was something Michel hadn't experienced in over two hundred years; it was something he could never experience.

Once again, I questioned what I had gotten myself into. No, *who* had I gotten myself involved with? He was centuries old. He wasn't human. He'd killed people in the past. And he was being hunted. And now I was also being hunted.

I sipped the tea as the sun sank lower on the horizon.

Should I have done something different last night? If I had never gone to him, I never would have ended up in this life-threatening situation. That would be the sensible thing to do.

But the idea of not being with Michel and missing out on all that had happened—the good and the bad—filled me with such a sense of loss I forced it from my mind.

My mind wandered from one memory to the next of the past day: speaking with Michel at Vamps, the explosion, the fire, the fighting, the drive up to Maine, his story, making love...

Just thinking about being with him made me miss his touch.

The last vestige of sun slipped into the ocean.

Ugh, what was I doing? Wrapping myself around a guy like this? This was not my style. Remembering I was a strong, independent woman, I put my tea on a table and walked down to the shore. I didn't need to have all my thoughts consumed by one man. I had a career, a family, friends, a life. And what about him? Could his existence even be called living?

I concentrated on the sensation of the cool October sand slipping through my toes. The ocean would be pretty cold by now at the final stretch of an Indian summer. Although I hated the cold water, I braved it and gasped when it hit my toes.

It'll pass in a minute. It's only the initial shock. I lost sense of time as I waded through the waters. Until I heard a man's voice.

"Well, well, well. Michel's little human came out to play in the waves."

The rest of my body froze with a chill that had nothing to do with the ocean. I turned to look and they were there. Both of them.

"What do you want?"

"Michel. Dead. What I've wanted for centuries."

"How can you still blame him? You were attacked and he defended the village the best he could with you."

"Silence," he said as he approached. "You have no business knowing my pain." His eyes blazed with fury. "Michel falling for you makes my vengeance all the sweeter."

"It's been centuries since your wife died. Time to get over it and move on."

"You are only a human, nothing but food, so he shouldn't have told you my affairs." He took a step closer and I could see his eyes reflect the moon, almost glowing like a cat's.

He had the same intense, bright eyes Michel had. While Michel's glance left me weak to my core, Ricard's left me with a much colder impression. Angry, cold, dead eyes.

"But you'll forget soon enough," he said. "Forget everything."

I took a step backward into the water. It wasn't the best of plans, but was better than running forward and straight into them.

"Imagine his torment when he finds your bloodless corpse on the beach and realizes what happened. I'll watch him grieve before I kill him."

"Stay away," I said, backing up deeper into the ocean.

He laughed. His beast companion laughed, too.

"You have nowhere to go. As if water would protect you. Humans," he said, shaking his head. "Stupid. Weak. Defenseless."

He was right, I had nowhere to go. But there were two ridiculously strong immortal freaks before me and I had to do something.

The water had reached my thighs. When the next wave approached, I dove, hoping it would help mask me and buy me some time. Time for what, I didn't know. To live?

It didn't. Ricard grabbed my ankle almost immediately and dragged me to the shore in seconds. I kicked, I tried to grab for things, but it was useless.

Ricard threw me on the shore as if I was as light as a seashell. For a brief flash, he and his little beast loomed over me. The beast's eyes frightened me even more than Ricard's. They reflected a yellow tinge, definitely not human.

Even worse was the stench. Apparently, they didn't practice hygiene. How could Michel have adapted to the modern times while these two were stuck in the past? Their trench coats dated to decades, maybe centuries, past.

When fangs pierced my neck, I screamed.

I tried to push them off, but it was futile, like pushing against concrete.

A groggy sensation came over me. The pain where they sucked from the wound had given way to a more soothing sensation. One that was somewhat sensual despite my revulsion. Although my senses were dulled, the knowledge that this vile creature were sucking my blood *and* turning me on against my will really pissed me off. I tried kicking them anywhere, everywhere, but it had no effect upon them.

Having my blood sucked from me by some gross, smelly vampires, or *nightwalkers* as they'd called themselves, seemed like a sucky way to die.

CHAPTER 6

M ichel Ricard had made a mess of my life in many ways. The physical damage to the club was only the beginning. Now I had employees' welfare to think about, insurance claims to deal with, and most importantly, a beautiful woman to protect. Strange how that compulsion dwarfed the others. For years, my businesses had been the most important things to me. Yet, with Nike being threatened—a woman I barely knew—something in my gut insisted keeping her safe was paramount.

After I hung up the phone from the last call I had to make, I rubbed my temples.

In a way, Ricard did me a favor. I was in a secluded cottage with a woman I'd wanted for ages. Alone together. What would have happened last night had he not blown up the club? Would we have gone home together? Made love?

Or would she have changed her mind and gone home alone? Impossible to know.

In a way, I wouldn't change a thing about last night.

Despite all the damage and destruction, spending the night with Nike was something I'd never regret.

Where was she now? On the deck? Funny how being apart from her, even for a little while, left a sort of ache inside. A yearning to be near her again.

I walked over to the back door to join her. That's when I discerned figures down near the water. A shudder ripped through me, culminating with a clenching of my gut. I rolled my hands into fists while my fangs protruded.

They had found us.

Ricard was crouched down over something, but the smaller one was blocking my view.

Where was Nike?

Before I could finish formulating the question in my head, I had figured it out. As I ran down to the shore, the predatory instinct to destroy them grew.

He better not have hurt her. She better be all right.

My vision was blinded by streaks of colors, mostly a crimson sheen that called for vengeance. I had to get to her before it was too late.

Nike

"Get off her!" Michel shouted.

When the weight was lifted off my torso, I gasped for breath, inhaling the scent of salt water. Michel was here. My heart thumped with an excited beat. *Michel came for me!*

Then, my relief vanished as quickly as if washed out by an ocean wave. Michel faced the two creatures. They moved closer to him, hunched over in a pose that screamed their intentions-- preparing to attack him. If their stance didn't convey it, the predatory hatred glaring in their eyes and pointed claws spelled it out like an insidious warning.

I was a human against these immortals, essentially helpless. With two of them against Michel, we were outnumbered.

Seagulls called as they flew overhead. Man, what I would give to be able to fly from this scene. But, I had to do something.

When I tried to stand, a dizzying sensation settled me back on my butt in the sand. Shit. I was too weak. As if being a human itself wasn't a disadvantage against supernatural beings, I now had to be a woozy human lightheaded from blood loss? Terrific.

Damn it! What could I do? How long could Michel fight the two of them off? If he went down, I'd go down next. We would both die at the hands of these wretched beasts. Our bodies might be thrown out into the sea. The possibility of someone finding us would be grim. My family, my friends, they'd be left to wonder. Was there anything worse than wondering the fate of your child? Whether they were dead or alive?

That's it. I had to do something to save us both, and keep my loved ones from suffering.

I crawled over the sand looking for something, *anything*, I could use to help. Bits of broken shells and stranded seaweed wouldn't help. Not standing helped with the wooziness.

A spray of warm liquid hit my arm. Blood had spattered over it. *Oh, dear hell.*

Ricard had a gash torn from his shoulder and Michel's mouth was bloody.

Ricard's blood. And maybe my blood, too. I gagged.

Shit. No. You're not going to puke. Focus!

Michel focused on the smaller one, who fought the way he looked—more beast than human. They lashed at each other, pounding the other's flesh with fists and baring teeth. Surely they would tear each other apart in no time.

Ricard recovered somewhat from the wound. He

approached the fierce circle and joined in, like a macabre version of *Ring around the Rosie.*

Which ended on an ominous final note with *We all fall down...*

Ricard contorted his body before launching onto Michel.

"Michel, watch out!" I screamed.

I crawled and grabbed some small rocks. I hurled them at Michel's opponents, careful not to hit him. They moved so quickly that I barely met the mark. The ones that hit them didn't seem to have any effect. Shit. That didn't help. I continued my search.

A longer piece of wood with a jagged edge was tangled in a pile of seaweed.

A stake?

Would it work? Damned if I knew. Before tonight, the only things I knew about vampires were from books and movies. I was the last person to discern fiction from fantasy. What other choice did I have but to try something?

Willing myself to ignore the dizziness and stand, I hoisted the stake over my head. With all the strength I could muster, I pinpointed my focus to Ricard's hunched over back. It crashed onto his frame, pierced the resistant flesh with a sickening tear through the tissue.

He howled, an inhuman sound that ended with an animal-like shriek. His skin smoldered around the wound. Ricard writhed on the dark sand like a demonic serpent, reaching for the makeshift stake. A vile, burning scent swamped the air.

Michel looked at me with wide eyes.

The smaller creature dove upon me and sank his teeth once again in my neck. Shit. I pounded at his back, yet the impact didn't alter anything. I'd already lost too much blood and as he drank from me with greedy slurps, my essence ebbed away.

Michel appeared over me and threw the smaller vampire aside. He grabbed the stake from Ricard's disintegrating back and stabbed the creature in his chest. His wound smoked with a ghastly scent of burning flesh. Michel yanked the stake again and plunged it into Ricard's chest this time.

"We have to make sure it pierces his heart," Michel said. "So he can't regenerate."

With the way Ricard's shrieks ceased and his body turned rigid, Michel's action appeared to have worked. The vile creature froze on hid back with limbs curled up toward the sky and fangs outstretch, like an oversized rat.

Their bodies blackened as they disintegrated, as if smoldering from the inside. The horrific scene transfixed me, leaving me unable to turn away, despite the revolting images that would haunt me. Within moments their bodies all but disappeared.

I turned to Michel. "They're gone?"

"Nothing but ashes."

I slid back to the sand to sit again and glanced at the waves that lapped the shore. High tide was approaching. They'd soon reach what remained of the corpses.

"Soon to be swept into the sea." A wave of weakness swept over me, leaving me wondering if the same fate awaited me if I didn't hurry up the shore. With this lack of energy, even the smallest amount of moving my limbs through water would be like swimming through hardening concrete.

Michel gathered some ash into his hand and let it sift through his fingers into the lapping waves. "Farewell, old friend. I hope you reunite with her in another world."

Forcing my eyes to stay opened to ensure that the ashes were in fact swept away, even that minute action became too difficult. My world darkened as if raven-winged shadows flew over me, blocking the stars and moon above.

"I'm sorry you had to go through that. It's all over now." His words sounded as if from a distance even though he was right next to me.

"Nike! Are you all right?"

I opened my mouth to answer, but even a response was more than I could manage.

"Nike," he repeated. "Stay with me. Oh God, they took too much from you." He pulled me onto his lap and my body felt laden by pebbles. "I don't want to do this. But *drink*."

He put his wrist to my lips and I tasted blood. I licked the blood from my lips and forced my eyes open to see him better.

"I don't want to…change."

"I won't give you much. Just enough. But, I've never done this before—and I don't want to lose you!"

I hesitated as I looked into his intense eyes, now a stormy blue filled with confusion and fear.

"Please," he implored. "It's the only way."

I opened my mouth to let the blood roll over my tongue. The unexpected sensation struck me as intimate. Michel's blood, his essence, flowed into me. Closing my eyes, I swallowed the copper honey.

The shadows moved in. The raven curtain fell over me and darkness reigned.

CHAPTER 7

Michel

"Nike, stay with me," I commanded, but she was out.

Fear rammed through me as sharply as a stake. She couldn't die. I wouldn't permit it!

I snorted. My desire meant nothing. Long ago, I'd discovered although I'd been cheating death for centuries, I couldn't prevent it from happening to others. Friends and loved ones grew to old age and died, while I lingered, continuing in this unnatural existence on this plane.

I carried Nike into the house and laid her on the bed. Wetting a face cloth with cool water, I wrung out the excess and placed it on her forehead. Focusing on bringing her some comfort helped me ignore the helplessness that wracked my body.

A glance at the mussed-up sheets filled me with despair. Had it only hours before when we'd slept in this bed intertwined? The passion we'd shared last night was supposed to be the beginning. Not the one and only time we would be together. The paleness of her face contrasted with the black sheets, which struck me as a terrible omen. Her face appeared too pale, too still. Too close to death.

I grabbed the closest thing that would shatter—a glass of water on the nightstand—and hurled it at the wall. The satisfying crash of glass breaking into dozens of shards only lasted a moment, followed by instant regret. Acting like a petulant child wouldn't save her.

Could it all end so soon? Before we even had a chance at trying?

I monitored her pulse. It was there, but faint. What could I do to help her? I'd given her some blood. Was it enough to help heal her?

Ignoring the shards of glass as I paced before her, I debated giving her more blood. What would it do?

What the hell would it do?

I didn't drain her of blood and flood her with mine to make her change. Cursing someone with my fate wasn't something I ever had the desire to do. I didn't want to start with Nike.

As long as she continued to breathe and had a pulse, I'd wait. Watch and wait. After all, as an immortal, I'd had plenty of practice in patience.

Her breath became heavier.

"Nike, can you hear me?"

Her eyes were still closed and she didn't respond. She turned onto her side and knocked the face cloth to the floor. Then she inhaled sharply.

I put a hand on her back to reassure her, even though I wasn't sure of anything myself. "You're going to be all right. I'm here with you."

Her mouth fell open as she gasped for air. Her throat contracted as she struggled to breathe.

What the fuck was happening to her?

In that moment, my feelings became clear. Despite all the

sensible notions that I shouldn't fall so hard for someone so soon. But to hell with sense, I knew it deep within.

She was the one for me. The only one. And if she pulled through, I would do whatever I could to be with her.

She had to make it.

Nike

Images flooded my mind, like I was caught in some surreal dream. Things that didn't make sense. Visions of people moving in ways that defied gravity, animals behaving in ways that defied logic for their species. Terrifying creatures like Ricard and his friend appeared, countering more sensual images of Michel. All this played out like a movie while pounding club music reverberated in my head. It was like I'd died and been reborn in a B horror flick.

Hours or maybe days later, I opened my eyes. The familiar outlines of the cozy cottage bedroom with a warm white down comforter reminded me where I was.

Had I turned into a vampire? Taking a quick assessment of my body for some odd signs, nothing indicated I'd changed somehow. If I went out into the sun, would I burn?

I pushed myself to sit up. "Michel?" I called out.

No answer. Where was he?

When I entered the main room of the cottage, it was empty. A quick glance outside the French doors onto the beach revealed that it was night. A tremble of fear shook through me as the last time I was out there flashed before in my mind. Yet, I didn't see any vampires, merely the innocent silhouette of a woman walking a golden retriever.

No Michel.

Hmm.

Before I went to find him, I figured I should wash the grime off my body. The echo of vampire blood might linger on my flesh, although it appeared to have been washed away.

I found a fluffy white bathrobe. In the shower, I turned the water up as hot as I could take it. The heat felt incredible against my skin. I could have stayed in there until all the hot water was gone. But concern for Michel forced me to speed up the pace. Was he coming back? Or had he left for good?

What about me? How did my body feel? Did I feel different?

The few cobwebs in my brain drifted away as I lathered my hair with a foamy shampoo. Then I tried to assess how I felt, head to toe. Although I'd felt beat up and sore the other night, now I didn't sense any pain.

I finished washing and rinsing and then stepped out, looking at myself in the bathroom mirror. Flashes of that erotic scene in front of the mirror with Michel invaded my thoughts. The way his lips felt against my neck. How his hand felt stroking against my skin.

Focus.

Were there any bruises? Cuts? No. Were they there before? Yes?

How long had I been out?

I towel dried my hair and body, put on the bathrobe and ran a brush through my hair.

What should I do next? Go look for him? If so, where?

I walked back into the bedroom. The bed was made with new sheets. My clothes were laid out on top. The scent of brewing coffee reached me. Oh, sweet heavens, what a welcome aroma.

When I walked out into the main area, the sight of him flooded me with an unfamiliar response. Relief. Solace. As if the universe had spun off kilter and had suddenly shifted back to its rightful position.

Michel's face brightened with a smile. "You're awake. How are you feeling?"

"Okay, I think. How about you?"

"Me?" He chuckled. "I'm fine. You're the one we need to worry about."

He strode over to me and I took in a sharp breath. How did he seem to suck up all the air in the room? He wrapped me in his arms.

"Mon amour."

I pressed my face against his chest, inhaling the scent of him. He was back. Or, I was. We were together.

He kissed me on the top of my head and then pulled back. Stepping over to the counter, he poured some coffee into an oversized mug. "Cream or sugar?"

"This is fine. Thanks."

I took a sip. The coffee was perfectly hot, so it almost burned, but the warmth was what I needed.

"Where were you when I was in the shower?" I asked.

"I ran to the store to pick up a few things."

"How long was I asleep for?"

"Come. Let's sit on the sofa."

He took my hand and led me to the living room. I put my coffee down on the end table. When we sat on the couch, he pulled me closer to him and I rested my head against his chest.

"You've been out almost forty-eight hours," he said. "It's been rough."

"How so?"

"The first several hours, you were breathing so erratically. I didn't know what was happening to you. Were you dying? Were you changing? Or were you just recovering from a traumatic experience?" He ran his hand over his chin. "It was brutal to see you like that and be helpless to do anything about it. I held your hand and hoped. And waited."

"Oh, that sounds awful," I said. "Waiting and wondering can drive you crazy. Your mind can go to some dark places."

He nodded. *"Exactment.* Around dawn, your breathing

evened out. Whatever was happening to you seemed to be settling down. Then you drifted into a deep sleep. I waited until I thought you were out of danger and then I held you in my arms and went to sleep. If anything happened to you, I wanted to be able to sense it."

My heart swelled. He held me all night. "Thank you for taking care of me."

"It was an honor." Michel put his hand on his heart. "At sunset, I woke up, but you were still sleeping peacefully. I ran out to pick up a few things in case we'd be here for a while longer for you to recover."

"Does this mean I'm out of danger?"

"I think so."

"Am I still me?"

"Of course."

"I mean—have I changed at all?"

"I don't know. How do you feel?"

I gauged how I felt once again. My body felt strong, not weakened by all that had happened.

"I don't feel a thirst for blood, if that's what you mean. But my wounds. They all healed so quickly. Overnight."

"Vampire blood might have helped with the healing." Michel's face contorted with conflict. "But, I don't know how the blood loss and then taking my blood will affect you. A vampire makes others by draining them of blood before replenishing their system. We didn't do that. To that level, at least."

The surreal dream was partially reality. I'd had my blood taken by a vampire and had drunk vampire blood myself. I took a sip of coffee to see if it tasted different. The hot liquid rolled over my tongue as if a magical salve; it reminded me of how Michel's blood had rolled over my tongue. I'd be lying if I didn't admit to being affected by it. What about my taste buds? Didn't vampires have super senses? The coffee tasted wondrous, but I chalked it up to the pleasure of a warm beverage after a traumatic experience, rather than some supernatural transformation.

Michel said, "What I do know is that I have fallen deeply for you. You came to my aid, against other immortals, when you could have run. You put yourself in danger for me. Not many are brave enough to risk that, especially for a stranger. I wish you'd never walked in the club that night, so you wouldn't have been involved in any of this danger. But that thought almost kills me. I want you with me. It may be self-ish, but that's how I feel. I want to take care of you and I want to protect you."

Whoa. Not even in my fantasies did I ever think I'd hear those words from the guy I longed for from afar at the rock climbing gym.

Then again, I never guessed he'd be a vampire, either.

He put a hand over mine. "When I thought I'd lose you…" He shook his head. "I'm torn. You'd be better off without me. But I want you. It's selfish of me, but I can't ignore how strong my feelings for you are."

I looked at his tormented face and wanted to reach out to him. "I don't understand everything that's happened. But what I know is that what I feel for you right now more than I've ever felt for anyone else. Everyone else—it seems like it was part of a game. Like it was pretend, or practice, for the real thing."

Michel gave me a warm smile and squeezed my thigh. "It isn't just me, then. You feel it, too?"

Taking a deep inhale, I admitted, "I do." So much had happened so quickly it was hard to understand. But my feel-ings were much clearer. "I didn't know supernatural things even existed before that night. I've seen a lot and I'm still trying to process it all. But, I do know I want to be with you."

He caressed my cheek and kissed me softly on the lips.

"Then we'll go through this together?"

I stared into his brilliant-blue eyes, at his sensuously carved lips. "Whatever happens. Yes, together."

Our lips met with a gentle kiss. It soon triggered an underlying yearning. Soft touching gave way to a more urgent union between our lips and tongues.

Michel pulled away from me. "I shouldn't. You're recovering."

I exhaled. The last thing I wanted right now was to be thwarted by sexual frustration. "I've rested for long enough, don't you think?" To solidify my point, I ran my hands over his torso.

He remained frozen for a second. "Nike," he whispered.

I loved the sound of my name coming from his lips.

Soon he put his hands on me again, roaming over my breasts and sides. He then lifted me and grabbed my ass over my robe with both hands, positioning me over his hips.

My robe slipped open beneath the waist as I lowered myself onto his lap. He was already growing hard beneath me.

"Ohhh." I moaned softly.

"That feels good," he replied. "So right."

As we kissed, I moved my hips down, pressing myself against his erection. He moaned this time. I worked myself up and down his shaft slowly, savoring the sensation of the growing heat between us.

"Are you all right, Nike? We shouldn't rush anything if you need rest."

"I need you," I said.

He grinned and it made my pulse quicken. "Then let's get these clothes off you."

"All I have on is this robe."

"The quicker I have you naked, the better."

He untied the belt around my waist and pushed the robe

off my shoulders. I pushed my arms back to let the robe fall down my arms. That action jutted my breasts forward.

"Oh, you're killing me," he said. He kissed down along my neck while one hand caressed my breast. Then he ran his tongue over to meet my other breast and encircled my nipple ever so gently.

"Now you're killing me," I said.

He took my nipple in his mouth. My head dropped back automatically in response to how good it felt.

He reached down and stroked between my legs. I was already wet, ready for more.

"Let's get you out of *your* clothes," I said.

I pulled the black fleece pullover over his head and then ran my hands over his chest. His chest and arms were defined. I smoothed the palm of my hands over his muscles. He watched me through those intense eyes as I undid his belt and unbuttoned and unzipped his black pants. He wasn't wearing underwear. For that, I was grateful.

I reached inside and stroked him, which made him drop his head back with a feral growl. That response, the way the mere touch of my hand made him react, encouraged me to continue. I inched his pants down his hips to expose more of him.

He stood and helped me to remove his pants, apparently just as desperate to clear the obstacles.

"Perfection," I said, admiring his muscled physique. Then I stood before him, naked and exposed, yet I didn't feel self-conscious around him.

We embraced again while we kissed, running our hands over each other's bodies, touching, exploring and caressing.

"This is so good," he murmured. "There are so many parts of you I want to touch I wish had more than two hands."

"I can be patient and wait while you get to all of them," I said.

"Good. Because I plan to explore you for a long, long time. I hope you don't have any plans to leave any time soon."

My mind flashed with the aftermath of that had happened. What would I tell Maya? My boss? That some creature sucked enough of my blood I almost died, but Michel was actually a supernatural creature himself and he let me drink his blood. That would go over *really* well.

"I can deal with reality tomorrow. Tonight is just for us."

"You've got that wrong," he said. When I furrowed my brow, he said, "Tonight is just the start of us. I don't want it to end."

"Then let's start it the right way. I can't wait for you much longer."

"So much for being patient," Michel teased. He picked me up and carried me into the bedroom, laying me on the bed. He kissed from my ankles up to my thighs. "You might want to work on the patience because I'm not going to rush any of what I have in mind."

He kissed my upper thighs and I quivered under the touch of his lips.

"You tease."

"I plan to." He nuzzled against my thigh and nibbled softly.

With a sigh, I dropped my head back on the pillow. "Don't make me wait too long."

"Don't you worry. I will make you appreciate how good things can be when you wait."

I reached down to stroke his cheek. "That sounds promising. I'm ready to be an attentive learner."

He moved up to kiss my neck and then hovered. The tips of his fangs peeked out from his lips. He appeared to struggle for self-control.

"Lesson one." He steeled himself with a determined expression. "Patience leads to great rewards."

AUTHOR'S NOTE

I hope you enjoyed the introduction to the Underground Encounters series with this novella. Maya's story is next in *Fire*, a novel that was named a Night Owl Reviews Top Pick!

"Lisa Carlisle has struck gold once again with "Fire" in her Underground Encounters Series. From the first page I couldn't stop reading. Tristan and Maya are both strong main characters that will make the reader laugh, cry, and sit on the edge of their seats."

"This book has it all-an adventure ride, hot and steamy scenes that will send one to a cold shower, laughs, some tears, but most of all a great story. Lisa Carlisle is a great author and she knows how to tell a great story." ~ Night Owl Reviews

"I don't want to spoil the story but let me say this... **you NEED to go and read this, NOW!"** ~ 5 Candles from Satin Sheets Romance.

Fire

Maya Winters, a firefighter, heads out on Halloween to dance at her favorite club. A man with haunting eyes watches her from the back of the club. **He's just her type–a dark,**

brooding bad boy. She feels their connection, but thinks it's merely physical attraction.

Despite being the new owner, Tristan Stone avoids people in the underground goth club due to his curse. But when he spots a woman dancing alone surrounded by an unusual glow, he must discover who she is and what gives her the radiating power.

While they work together to understand their connection, passion ignites, leading to danger. **And the heat could send their world up in flames.**

Fire is book 2 in the Underground Encounters series, set in a club that attracts supernatural creatures. *Step into Vamps, a thrilling new world of steamy paranormal romance featuring sexy shifters, thirsty vampires, wicked witches, and gorgeous gargoyles.*

Maya

I hadn't been back since the fire.

Whoever had bought the club had kept the black brick exterior with the painted black windows, ensconcing the club in mystery. Passersby down this hidden alley might think it an abandoned warehouse, unless they got close enough to look up into the recessed doorway to see it flanked by two watchful gargoyle statues.

A moment of hesitation filled me. When I would come with my best friend Nike, I'd never felt threatened. We'd come after long shifts at the firehouse to unwind and dance off some steam. I'd practically bounce down the alleyway so I could get inside sooner.

But now, on my own, the creepiness of the alleyway set in. I wrapped my long black leather trench coat tightly around my body to shield my fishnet-covered legs as if protecting myself. It could be dangerous walking alone through warehouse alleys near the waterfront. No wonder Vamps was hidden back here. You wouldn't want an underground club on the main drag, would you?

My Mary Jane heels clicked loudly on the cement. The further I walked, the closer the clicks were.

Easy, Maya, I chastised myself. *You're going to break into a trot in a second.*

Finally, I made it to the front entrance and pulled on the heavy wooden doors with steel bars intersecting in the middle and was rewarded by a familiar figure.

"Byron, you're still here!" I said to the extra-large bouncer who had an extra-large heart.

"Maya, where have ya been?" He threw his enormous arms wide and I rushed in, aware that I was grabbing him tighter than warranted, probably due to relief after my misgivings walking here alone.

"Whoa, girl, you must have really missed me," he said before he let me go.

"Of course I did. It's been forever. How have you been?"

"Survivin'. Taking odd jobs here and there while they rebuilt this place. You saw the damage from the explosion."

"Yes, I remember." It wasn't something I could forget any time soon.

"Why you here alone tonight?" he asked. "Where's your partner in crime?"

"Nike? I haven't seen her since the fire."

"Are you kidding me? It's been what—a year?" After I nodded, he asked, "What happened with her then? One of the bartenders told me how she saw her go upstairs with the former owner that night. What do you—they hooked up?"

I didn't know how much to tell about Nike and Michel,

even though I was still hurt that I hadn't seen her. Sure, she sent brief emails from time to time, letting me know which country they were in, but it wasn't the same. We were like this—if you could see me, you'd know I was wrapping my index and middle fingers together. Byron was concerned about her, but I also didn't want to perpetuate any rumors.

"Word spreads quickly around here, doesn't it?" I chose to avoid the juicy part of the question and answered, "Last I heard she was traveling around Europe." I left out the part that she was with Michel.

We were interrupted by a couple who opened the door. He was wearing a red velvet smoking jacket a la Gomez Addams, but didn't pull off the look completely with his dirty-blond hair. While they showed their IDs to Byron and paid the cover charge, I glanced at her outfit to see if she was sporting a Morticia-like dress. To my surprise, she was wearing a cowgirl outfit—hat, tassels, boots, and a short shirt. Not a usual costume for a goth club, but she pulled it off.

Note to self: see if you can pull off a sexy cowgirl outfit.

After they passed through the next set of doors, Byron asked, "So you're solo tonight?"

"Hopefully not all night," I lifted an eyebrow. "How's the eye candy in there?"

"You know, the usual. Lots of weirdos."

"Just my type."

"Who you kiddin'? I've never seen you leave with anyone besides your girl Nike."

"Byron. I haven't been out in months. I went on some crappy dates this past year and realized I'm happier just being on my own. All I've done lately is work. Which means the only males I've encountered are coworkers and they smell pretty rank after a twenty-four-hour shift. Since Halloween is on a Saturday this year, and Halloween was always the best night of the year here, I decided to climb out of my self-imposed isolation and make an appearance."

"Well then, get in there and be a naughty girl." Byron smacked me playfully on the ass to push me on. Then he said, "Wait." He took my hands and extended them out to the side. "Let me get a good look at you. See what outfit you're sporting tonight. Are you wearing a costume under there?"

I cocked my head as I took my hands back to open my leather trench coat shawl, which could fit in just perfectly at a gothic club or a Renaissance fair, but not too many other places. Tonight I was wearing a sexy little pirate wench costume, with a laced-up corset top and short leather miniskirt. "Does this warrant your approval?"

He put his hand on his chin as he sized me up. "Not bad. I've seen you in worse. Still trying to forget the blue velvet gown, black combat boots debacle."

"That was hot," I protested.

He raised an eyebrow before his gaze moved up to my hair. "And you've gone back to black hair, I see?"

"Technically blue-black. There's only so much color I can get away with at work, being a professional and all." I winked. Lately, I'd been alternating between blue-black and a magenta tint, which was about as much as I could manage without the fire chief giving me the look. If I was feeling spunky and wanted to sport a hot pink or blue, I'd wear a wig.

"All right, you get my seal of approval. And you know that's not so easy, princess. Go on in."

I kissed him on the cheek and walked down the dark tunnel lit by candelabras attached to the stone walls. A new sign adorned the door leading to the main club area. Dante's quote was carved into the wood: *Abandon Hope All Ye Who Enter Here.*

"But Maya," he called after me. "Leave some of the pretty boys for me."

"Obviously," I said, with an exaggerated eye roll. "Not my style."

~

MUCH OF VAMPS looked the same, yet much of it had changed. Gargoyles still guarded from their perches around the club. The three smaller dance platforms were replaced by one larger stage. They now had live bands perform up there as indicated by posters adorning the walls. Or when the stage was free as it was now, it was covered with uninhibited dancers who wanted to be watched.

I worried the vibe of the club wouldn't survive the transition. Some clubs try too hard and end up seeming phony. Vamps always had its own style. Some called it goth for the prevalence of goth-inspired dress and music. But they played other music as well. Others called it a fetish club for the revealing leather or vinyl outfits many chose to wear. Black duct tape pasted over nipples has been seen more than once. And the sexy futuristic outfits with hulking boots were a common choice. But to me a fetish club alluded to sex out in the open, which wasn't the case here. I'd never caught anyone doing it—but I have seen some couples get pretty close on the dance floor or in a corner.

I'd call it more of an underground club. One that was frequented by people who didn't stick to conventional dress and music and followed their own path, rather than worrying what other people thought. Whatever the club was, it was where I fit in.

Continuing to look around and assess the club, I thought it still had an authentic feel. The red marble bar hadn't survived the fire, I noted. But it was still manned—or womanned—by the hot bartender with pink hair and a nice rack. I looked over the drink menu posted above the draft beer.

"What's in a Tempting Fate?" I asked her.

"Southern Comfort, Amaretto, vodka, pomegranate juice, pineapple juice, grenadine," she rolled out in a velvety voice that was as sexy as she was.

"Sold," I said, banging an imaginary gavel.

"You won't regret it," she said.

After she gave me my drink, I toasted nobody in particular, well, I guess myself. *Here's to tempting fate.* I watched the crowd as I tasted the drink. It was exquisite and I took another large sip. Maybe I'd pay for it tomorrow, but it was *gooood.*

When I heard a remix of Type O Negative's *Cinnamon Girl*, I left my drink at the bar to slink my way amid the gyrating bodies. My favorite band, one of my favorite songs. Tragic that the super-hot singer died so young.

In a sea of black-clad bodies, I blended right in. It had been months since I danced, but I quickly found my rhythm and lost myself in the music, dancing with the crowd. I didn't feel the least bit self-conscious that I was alone.

That is—until I felt his eyes on me.

You know the feeling when someone is watching you and you're suddenly aware of it? That tingling sensation made me look up. A tall guy dressed all in black—naturally—stood alone at the right side of the bar.

Something about that gaze arrested me and I stopped dancing. Dark eyes, almost black, on a face that looked as captivating as Jim Morrison in the Young Lion photo shoot. The black hair was a devil-may-care length, past his chin but not quite to his shoulders. Instead of the rock star's signature black leather pants, this guy was wearing a cape over dark clothing.

His gaze penetrated me. So intense. The eyes of someone who was troubled—maybe haunted.

Why was he staring at me like that? Didn't he know my weakness was a dark, brooding bad boy?

My lips parted as if they wanted to say something. But what did I want to say? And he couldn't hear me anyway.

And then with a swoop of his cape, he was gone.

I stood there for a few more moments trying to process what just happened. Some hot guy in the corner watched me, who then took off with a flourish of his cape?

It seemed very Bela Lugosi-ish—another dark, brooding bad boy. I tried to shake off my confusion as *Cinnamon Girl* ended.

The DJ mixed in a version of David Bowie and Trent Reznor's *I'm Afraid of Americans*. It took me another moment or two to brush off the effect that dark stranger had on me. I thought *to hell with that guy* and then got back into my groove.

Tristan

Although I usually worked in the lab while the club was open, an industrial remix of *Strange Days* by the Doors snapped me out of my project. I couldn't hide out down here all night; time to make sure business was running smoothly upstairs.

Bracing myself for the onslaught on my psyche, I took a deep breath before I walked into the main club area. I glanced around the perimeter of the club, scanning the bar area and the dance floor.

The usual darkness surrounded people, the sadness, the isolation, which I could see so vividly while others couldn't.

Their souls crying out to me, draining me. I tried to ignore their pull as I glanced around. The bartenders looked busy. The bouncers looked alert for any drunken jerks acting out of control. The gargoyle statues stood intact, watching over the club from their perches. Their stone eyes could see more than they let on. I'd never seen these guards in their human form, yet heard they'd shift at the sign of danger.

Nothing seemed amiss. Good, I could make my rounds and get out of there and back to the lab.

But then one figure on the dance floor caught my eye. She glowed with a light around her unlike any I'd encountered before. Her bright spirit overwhelmed the darkness that surrounded the others. I watched as she danced, oblivious to those around her. Her light mesmerized me. For the first time I'd been around people other than my family, I wasn't overwhelmed by darkness.

I couldn't take my eyes off her. What was it she had?

Then she stopped and looked at me. Even though the club was dark, her light revealed her eyes were a brilliant blue.

When our eyes met, I saw her more clearly. A sadness buried deep within this bright spirit. Whereas others' pain usually repelled me, her pain filled me with compassion. What was hiding there so deeply within this light? What hurt her? Suddenly I wanted to protect her from any pain.

Her light was magnetic; it drew me in. Now that her captivating eyes were staring back at me as well, I became unnerved.

I turned away and disappeared down the back stairwell. Safely in my lab, I sat in my leather chair in the corner I dubbed the library and thought.

What was she?

What would explain the light?

I scanned the books in the library, on the bookshelves

built into a rounded wall modeled after one I admired in nearby Hammond Castle. I had books and books on the supernatural, so I flipped through them trying to find more information on why I saw what I did and what that meant.

I flipped through one book after another, reading by the light from the candelabra, which I found more soothing than artificial light.

What would explain what I just saw upstairs with that woman? Finding nothing, I closed the book and stared into the flames. Then I closed my eyes.

A vision of her dancing quickly shaped itself in my mind's eye. Getting past the initial shock of her light, I remembered the way she moved, the way she danced unabashed to *Cinnamon Girl*. I saw her hips sway, her arms unfurl into the air as if conjuring up the elements, her black hair wave out behind her as she tossed her head back. I visualized her long legs extend up from those chunky black heels, up, up to the tiniest of skirts in her pirate wench costume. Who wouldn't want a peek?

My curiosity about her was now piqued by my arousal. I felt consumed with a need to see her again. What was she like? I had to get up there and meet her.

I blew out the candles and went upstairs, returning to the dance floor area where I'd last seen her. She wasn't there any longer. I walked the perimeter of the dance floor, looking for her.

Where was she? She should be easy to see with that light. That glow.

Was it gone? Was it just my mind playing tricks on me?

Yes, that would explain it. I'd never seen anything like that before. It couldn't be real. It shouldn't be.

Nevertheless, I scanned the people at the bar looking for my little pirate wench. But she was nowhere to be seen.

I exhaled with a deep sigh of regret. I blew it.

Maya

An hour or two later, I decided my dancing legs were broken back in and were now ready for a rest. I went to the ladies' room to make sure I didn't acquire raccoon eyes working up a sweat out there, retrieved my leather trench coat from coat check, and then pulled a heavy door to walk back up the alley.

Byron was talking to someone dressed all in black. The man's back was toward me and I quickly noted the slightly long black hair on a tall frame like Peter Steele of Type O Negative, at least 6' 3".

Yes, this was a good night to come back.

Although he was wearing a dark cape, I noted his broad shoulders. Capes were donned by many Halloween revelers tonight, much like my recent encounter with that dark-eyed mystery man. Who just happened to be tall, dark, and caped.

Byron caught my eye. "You're not leaving already, are you? It's far too early to call it a night."

"I think I've had enough, Byron. Looks as if I need to break in slowly."

"Mr. Stone, this is Maya. She used to be a regular at the old club. It's her first time back since you reopened it."

When this Mr. Stone turned to me, my insides flipped as if acrobats set up a circus routine. Holy shit, it was the guy who stared at me on the dance floor. The one who gave me weird heart palpitations.

Our gazes caught. His dark, penetrating stare did something to me. Something weird. I was aware of this thing beating frantically inside my chest. How difficult it was to swallow.

Why couldn't I break our stare? That connection was too intense.

"A pleasure," he said. I wasn't expecting such a deep voice, as sexy as Alan Rickman's but with the accent of someone who grew up on the North Shore. Amazing how a sexy accent can affect your reaction to the opposite sex.

He bowed slightly to take my hand and kiss it. The tingle that shot from his hand on mine, his lips on my skin, did something to me that I still can't logically explain.

It really must have been too long since I'd been out and interacting with the male species.

"Mr. Stone is the new owner," Byron explained. "He put a lot of attention into rebuilding the club."

"And you're leaving so soon?" he said, never breaking our gaze. "What a shame. I hope it's not that the club doesn't live up to your expectations."

Several seconds passed while my eyes traveled from his dark ones down to stare at lips that I could kiss for days —"interface with," as the guys at work said when geeking out talking about girls. Suddenly aware that I still hadn't uttered a word, I said, "No, it's not that, Mr. Stone. It looks great. I don't want to overdo it. Haven't used these dancing legs in a long time."

"Please call me Tristan. Come, Maya, I'm not convinced. Let me show you around. Maybe get a drink. I'd love to get input from a former regular to see if we're missing any of the old charm."

He took my hand and warmth once again spread from where he touched me all through my body. I controlled my racing pulse for a moment to turn back and look at Byron. His mouth was half-open in shock, but then he recovered in time to wag his finger in front of his face with a naughty grin.

I shrugged back at Byron before Tristan reopened one of the doors into the main club area leading us back into Dante's Inferno as hinted at by the sign. Tristan led me into the loud music and pulsing energy in the club. What was I getting into?

He pointed out some of the new features of the club, the new live stage and a newer bar. Polished black marble graced the top of a dark mahogany carved-wood bar, with scenes of ancient rites of what looked like naked witches dancing around a cauldron carved into the front panels.

We walked over to the bar and he asked, "What would you like to drink?"

"I tried a Tempting Fate earlier and it was smashing." I tilted my head and peered up at him. "Anything else on the menu you'd recommend?"

He stepped back and looked at me. No, appraised me up and down in an unabashed manner. If another guy looked at me that way, I'd rip him a new one, but when Tristan did it, it made me blush. Set me on fire.

I didn't blush often and I wondered why I did now. Luckily it was dark in here.

"I think you deserve a drink as delectable as you look. But that might be hard to concoct. How about a Hotter Than Hell Bloody Mary?"

"Aren't you a flatterer," I said, aware that I was fluttering my lashes like some flirt. "Do you use that line on all the females here?"

"Never before. Boy Scout honor."

I tilted my head. "Were you a Boy Scout?"

"No. Does that matter?"

I shrugged and took a sip of my drink. "Excellent choice," I said. I looked around the club. "I like what you've done with the place. The little touches make it unique. And the new drinks are extraordinary."

"Thank you."

"No, thank you for buying the club. Saving the place."

Seeing all the people on the dance floor, I added, "You've made a lot of people happy."

"I hope you're one of them." He looked at me so intensely that I felt self-conscious.

"I am. This is my favorite place for a night out."

"I'm glad to hear that," he said. "The live music is what I think will really give this place a new life. We had an old punk band in here last week. Wicked fun. You'll have to come and judge for yourself one night."

"I will," I said. As if I needed another reason to come back. First, this was my number one choice for a night out. Second, the new owner's penetrating eyes and his special attention on me right now reminded me of forgotten body parts that had been out of commission for far too long. And third, I loved live music.

Digital music was one thing. It was convenient and you could listen to just about anything you wanted. Records were cooler. That crackly sound and delicate vinyl gave it a sense of something special in a way. But live music—when you could hear the music surrounding you from all angles so that you could practically taste it. When you could see the sweat glistening on the guitar player's forehead and feel his passion for his song. When you caught the energy of the crowd and jumped or danced with them like some kind of collective orgy experience, well, nothing could replace that.

"Wicked?" I asked. "You must be local. We didn't use that expression where I grew up and I only heard it when I moved here."

"I'm from Salem, originally. But now I live near the club."

"Salem, Mass, right? Not New Hampshire," I said. "We're kind of between them both."

"Yes, Massachusetts. Good ol' Witch City," he said. "Where are you from?"

"San Francisco. I'm a California girl, can't you tell?" I said with a grin. With my Bettie Page-styled black hair and straight bangs, pale skin, and goth makeup, I was as opposite of a stereotypical California girl as could be.

"You're what I hope they all look like."

I looked down again. Why did he keep making me blush? This was not something I did often.

"What made you decide to buy this club?" I asked, changing the subject.

"Every area needs someplace for the people who don't quite fit in with the traditional boring people who all act the same."

"Would you say you don't fit in with the norm?"

He gave me an impish smile and raised one brow. "God, no." Then he said, "Look what happened to that club in Cambridge. Gone. Replaced by condos. I didn't want to see that happen to this place—have it disappear and be replaced by yet another condo or warehouse."

I looked around the club to imagine it divided into condos that all looked the same.

"That would have been tragic," I said. "On behalf of all the misfits here, I thank you."

He smiled at me in a way that shot pulses of energy through my body. I took a sip of my drink to break the gaze.

"I better get going," I said, standing up. "Thank you for the tour. And for reopening Vamps. I love what you've done with it."

"Let me walk you out," he said. He stood and took my hand in his and led me to the front entrance.

The feel of my hand encased in his warm one did nothing to stop my racing heartbeat.

"Did you drive? Or should I call you a taxi?" he asked.

"A taxi would be great."

While he placed a quick call, I said goodbye to Byron. He gave me a knowing smile, which I ignored. Tristan took my hand again and led me outside.

"It was such a pleasure meeting you, Maya."

"Same here," I said, feeling pangs of regret for saying I had to leave.

The regret was amplified when the stupid taxi arrived and Tristan kissed my hand.

"I hope to see you again very soon."

When I closed my eyes that night, I saw Tristan's dark eyes staring back at me. The moment when my eyes first met his burned on my memory, as if imprinted there permanently. I wouldn't forget that moment, that feeling, for as long as I'd exist.

Snap out of it, sunshine. You sound like you're in a romance novel.

Then I thought, *What's the harm? I'm awake. I can't sleep. What's wrong with a little harmless fantasy? When was the last time I met someone who inspired such longing? Or straight-out lust?*

I tucked myself in cozy under my pale blue comforter and closed my eyes.

Tristan and I were at Vamps. We were dancing to an upbeat song. *Hard Rock Sofa* by Quasar. Our eyes were locked on each other's, oblivious to the dancing bodies around us.

As the tempo quickened, the crowd's energy rose around us, becoming more and intense, almost frenzied. Our bodies moved closer. Still we didn't touch.

My body was so hot, on fire. Was it from dancing, the energy of the crowd? Or the rising intensity of how badly I wanted Tristan?

We moved closer still. Faces mere inches apart. Eyes still locked. Bodies almost touching.

Almost.

The tempo grew faster. To a feverish intensity.

Closer still. I broke eye contact to look at his lips. Licked my own.

God, I wanted to touch him. Kiss those lips.

The beat was at a peak now. Almost orgasmic.

I looked back into his eyes and saw pure, unmistakable lust.

Touch me, my body screamed silently. Touch me now.

The crescendo broke. And with it, the crowd lost all control, their sweaty bodies flailing about to dance freely.

We followed them. And our bodies moved apart to dance. A wanton, seductive dance.

When the song ended, the DJ spun in a slower one.

Our eyes met again. Our bodies moved closer again. One hand reached toward me. I closed my eyes. Then I felt his hand on the small of my back. Pulling me close. Closer.

A song began playing over this one. It sounded so familiar. What was it?

Oh yeah, it's Black No. 1, a great Type O Negative song.

I should have recognized it right away—it was my cell phone ringtone.

Fuck, it was my cell phone ringing.

Who the hell would call at this ungodly hour?

"Hel-*lo*," I said, making sure the annoyance was apparent in my tone.

Double fuck. It was one of the guys at the firehouse.

"We're short-staffed tonight. Figures, on Halloween. Can you come in for a few hours?"

"It's after midnight. Not Halloween anymore."

"Yeah, but I knew you'd still be up."

I could use the overtime. Pushing my fantasy aside, I sighed before hopping into a shower of the coldest water I could stand.

One thing was clear. I had to see Tristan Stone again.

Tristan

Days had passed. I asked myself the same question repeatedly: Why did I let her go?

I ruminated in my lab, running my hands over a marble globe on an end table. I spun it, letting the cool feel of the marble glide under my fingers and closed my eyes. Then I stopped it.

My fingers were in the middle of the Atlantic. Might as well have been in the middle of nowhere.

I should have at least asked for her number or a way to contact her again. Instead, I kept an eye out for her at the club each night it was open, but she wasn't there. Why should I entertain false hope that she'd return? I hadn't seen her there before Halloween night. And there she appeared to me in that light—a vixen dressed like a pirate.

What did she look like in everyday clothes? And would she ever return?

Swallowing some pride, I went upstairs.

"Byron, has your friend returned lately? Maya, is it?" I said.

Byron gave me a knowing smile, which he quickly recovered from. "No, only that one time since the club reopened."

"What can you tell me about her?"

Byron ran his finger over his chin. "I don't know her that well. We would talk when she'd come in with her friend Nike some nights. They both helped get people out the night of the fire. I think they work in some sort of emergency services field or something because they seemed to know what they were doing. And that was the last time I saw either one of them until Maya came back."

"Interesting," I said.

"Why do you ask?"

"I want to talk to her."

Byron smiled that smile again, this time not trying to hide the twinkle in his gaze. "If I see her, I'll be sure to tell her."

Maya

I thought about Tristan all week. Not even the banter with the guys at the firehouse kept him too far from my mind. Luckily, it was a busy week. I had to teach fire prevention and safety to an elementary school and we had a visit from a Cub Scout troop, in addition to the usual calls.

Every night I wanted to go back to Vamps. Would I still feel that excitement that welled up when I was around him? The one that made me hyperaware of my sexuality?

I pictured him walking around the perimeter of the club. I checked the website once to see what was going on. Okay, three times. Any live bands playing? Maybe some band I was dying to see that just happened to be playing there tonight so naturally I would go there to see them. I definitely was *not* there hoping to see the new owner who just happened to be ridiculously attractive.

What about all the women parading around in their tiny, sexy outfits? Usually I loved checking out what everyone was wearing. I never went to Vamps to date so a jealous thought never entered my mind. But now I pouted thinking of all those hot women who would just love to sleep with the new owner.

Damn sluts!

Stop it. What's gotten into you? You sound like some jealous stalker.

Obviously, I needed some distance because even in my head I was already going crazy over this guy. If I stayed away, maybe I'd forget him.

At times like this, I wish Nike was still around instead of

gallivanting around Europe doing whatever she was doing with Michel and his perfect ooh-la-la French accent.

I mean, come on. Who else could I talk about this with? I was certainly *not* going to talk about it with the guys at work.

Woe is me, I thought, knowing I was being dramatic. I put the back of my hand against my forehead as I looked at myself in the mirror.

"How sad are you right now?" I said to my reflection.

Settling into my sofa, I grabbed my iPad to compose an e-mail to Nike. Our emails had been brief since she'd left, since I was still hurt about her minimal communication. But I needed someone to talk to and Nike was still my closest friend, even though she was across the ocean or wherever the hell she was these days.

Hey Nike,

How are you doing? I haven't talked to you in so long and it sucks. I miss you big time.

Are you and Michel getting it on all over Europe? On the Eiffel Tower? Leaning off the Tower of Pisa, perhaps? Ha ha.

I can't believe I haven't seen you since last year, on the night of the fire. I went back to Vamps for the first time this Halloween. Byron was there at the front door. He asked about you and says hi. The new owner rebuilt it well. He kept much of the old charm, but rebuilt the stages differently so they can have live bands now. That's pretty cool, I think. Anyway, thought you'd be interested in our old haunt. And Michel would be interested in his old club.

So, I met the new owner. A guy named Tristan Stone. Tall, dark and ridiculous handsome stranger. Totally my cup of tea. I hate to admit it, but I think I'm smitten. Preposterous after just one conversation, isn't it? Go ahead and slap me back to reality.

But something about him—I don't know how to describe it—but I can't stop thinking about him. I know, it sounds cheesy. But maybe you know what I mean. You turned into jelly when you saw

Michel at Vamps that night, not your normal tough-ass self. What is it about us and owners of this club making us forget all reason? Does an irresistible love potion come with the deed?

I don't know if you'll even get this. If you have access to e-mail wherever you are these days. But I just wanted you to know I miss you. And you were the one person I could talk to about things like this.

And to confess how I feel like some psycho stalker because I can't wait to go back and see him again. As if he'd even remember me. Just another visitor to the club. Obviously I need to get a grip.

I hope things are great with you and we'll see each other again soon. Any idea when you're coming home?

Are you coming home?

Maya

I signed out of my e-mail and went to bed. I crawled under my comforter and tried not to think of him.

As I drifted off to sleep, I saw his eyes. Those dark haunted eyes that were imprinted on me. Would I ever forget them?

Tristan

None of my books answered any of the questions about Maya's light. So, I drove to Salem to have lunch with someone who might—my mother.

We sat down in her dining area with large windows showing off her gardens. Although it was early November in New England and the flowers were gone, Mother ensured she would have the most of her gardens for as much of the year as she could. She called the garden her incomplete canvas, one that she'd redesign throughout the seasons. Brilliant reds of Japanese maples and other perennials now dominated the landscape.

We discussed family matters over light sandwiches that

Charlotte brought out. Mother had hired Charlotte in recent months to help her around the house, saying it was too much for her to take care of on her own anymore. Charlotte had lost her husband and looked for a job to keep her mind focused on something besides mourning.

Following the meal, Charlotte brought us tea. Tea was a daily ritual in my parents' house. Mother used it as her salve for all life's matters, her quiet meditation throughout the madness of any day.

"Tristan, something is troubling you. I could sense it since you came in."

I wanted to tell her about Maya, but didn't know where to begin. "Yes, Mother. Something is on my mind. Something I don't understand."

"What is it?" she asked and took a sip of tea.

"It's a woman."

My mother leaned forward, smiling. She'd wanted me to settle down and get married for ages, so any mention of a female had her imagination spiraling. But with my ability, whatever it was, I wasn't a good companion for another person.

"Go on," she encouraged.

"She came into my club the other night. There was something about her that I've never seen before."

"What?"

"She was surrounded by a soft white light. Where all I saw around other people were the usual darkness and shadows, she projected this—glow."

Mother looked me in the eyes for several long moments. I looked down at my tea, which was still untouched.

"Interesting," Mother said. "What happened to the darkness?"

I tried to remember. "I'm not sure exactly. I don't know if it was still there. I was so focused on her that I didn't notice."

"Next time you see her pay attention to what happens."

"I don't know if I'll see her again."

"But Tristan," she said touching my hand, "you must."

"Why?"

"Obviously something special happened between you two. And considering your gift."

"Curse," I corrected.

She ignored my correction.

"It means something. It's something worth pursuing."

"What do you think it is?"

"I don't know," she said. "Drink your tea and I'll read the leaves. Maybe we'll find some insight there."

We drank our tea in silence, caught up in our thoughts. I thought of Maya the whole time. I tipped the cup upside down when I was done so the leaves could slide down the china, leaving a trail as they descended. My mother looked upon these markings as foretelling the future. I'd stopped questioning her method long ago.

"While we wait, let's do a reading," she said.

"Not a full one," I said. "Just one card." She shuffled the cards skillfully as she'd done this hundreds of times. "I wish my gift was similar to yours—how nice must it be to tell people their good fortune."

She looked at me over her Tarot deck. "It's not all hearts and flowers. Most of the time when people come to me, it's because they're troubled. And much of the time, when I read for them, they have reason to be. It's not that easy to see that their worst fears may be imminent and yet try to focus on the positive. Try to help them find a way out of their predicament."

"The difference is that you choose to meet with people. You can help them. I *don't want* this ability. What good is it to see sadness in people? I can't do anything about it! I don't want to see their pain." Why was I raising my voice right now? And bringing up a topic I hated to discuss with her?

"Tristan," she said in a soothing voice. "Some gifts take more time to develop than others. Especially if the person fights it. Maybe someday you'll find what makes your ability so special. Our paths are not always clear at first and you're still so young."

I bit my tongue to stop the retort forming and let her do her thing.

"One day you will do great things. I know this."

"Of course you think that. You're my mother. Nobody else feels that way about me. Especially not me."

She looked at me with a mother's sympathy. Then she said, "Close your eyes. Focus on your concern."

I closed my eyes and thought of Maya and her light. Then I picked a card.

"The Emperor," she said. "Major arcana." She looked up at me. "You want to find some influence over things you have no control over. You're thinking about her; she's thinking about you. You will spend much time together. Working together—maybe having fun together. Ultimately, you must work with her to achieve your desires."

"This is ridiculous," I said, pushing my chair back. "I'm not buying it. I might be wondering about her, but she is most definitely *not* thinking about me. Why would she? And I have been alone for almost thirty years. Someone is not going to walk into my life now and change everything just because of what you see on some card."

She just smiled at me and picked up my tea cup to examine the leaves. She turned the cup around slowly and humphed here and there.

"What is it?"

"I'm not sure," she said and looked up at me. "Can you bring her here?"

"Bring her here? I don't even know how to contact her. Why on earth would I bring her here?

She put down the cup and looked me straight in the eye. "I want to meet her."

Maya

One week went by. Saturday night. I wished I was spending my evening getting ready to go to Vamps and seduce one Mr. Tristan "Smoking-Hot Guy" Stone. But I was a working girl. So instead, I sat around in a firehouse, the only female working with a bunch of guys. Although I was usually one of the first ones to engage in the friendly banter that kept us entertained during the dragging moments, lately I was distracted by other things.

Bob Walker, a middle-aged firefighter, noticed I wasn't my perky old self. After most of the guys went out on a call and it was only the two of us left, he asked, "What's with you lately? Most people can barely get a word in when you're around. You haven't said two sentences in a row all week."

"Things on my mind. You know, things."

"I know what that means," he said with a smirk. "I have two teenage daughters. I don't need a crystal ball to see that by 'things' you mean a guy."

I frowned. So much for keeping my angst to myself.

"Do you want to tell me about it?" he asked.

As a matter of fact, I would have liked to spew out all the racing thoughts in my brain to someone who would just listen to me ramble. But then that would require spilling the beans on the part of my life where I liked to dress in sexy outfits and go to underground clubs. And that would not go down well in a firehouse full of guys, for me at least. Endless ribbing and inappropriate questions would ensue.

"Thanks, but there's nothing to tell."

A couple of emergency calls distracted me during my

shift. An old woman who was having trouble breathing had to be taken by ambulance to the hospital. Also, a teenager who was freaking out on drugs had to go in.

Another week went by. I had two days off in a row midweek. I checked the club's website once, okay every day, to see what was going on, but then reminded myself to snap out of it. Instead I spent one night having dinner catching up with a friend and the other one going to the movies on my own.

Saturday night finally came again. Whenever Nike and I had Saturday nights off, we'd go to Vamps as it was the best night of the week. I wished she was with me now for some moral support at least, but there was someone else I wanted to see that night even more.

I paid particular attention to my appearance that evening. After a long, hot shower where I groomed myself as meticulously as if I had a lover awaiting me that evening, I then spent another forty-five minutes trying on outfits. One by one they went from my closet to my body, and then after being rejected, tossed onto an armchair.

"Ugh, stop acting as if you're in middle school and just pick something," I admonished myself.

Finally, I decided on a form-fitting black dress, with Asian red floral satin accents down the front and back where the dress laced together and a slit that reached halfway up my thigh. Sure the black would blend in with everyone else, but the red gave it a little punch. And I wanted to be seen by someone in particular. Not stand out in a bright red, look-at-me, va-va-va-voom number, but one that gave me a little differentiation from the crowd.

I straightened my still-black hair until it went halfway down my back and then gave it a little curl at the ends with a fat curling iron. I ironed my bangs straight, Bettie Page-style.

Then I was extra careful making my face up. I lined my blue eyes with black eyeliner to set them off and used plenty of mascara, then softened them with a smoky gray eye shadow. Lipstick tonight called for fire-engine-red. In order to act like a seductress, I had to look like one. And the first person I had to convince was myself.

I looked in the mirror and smiled. For someone who'd been sporting firefighting uniforms or schlepping around in lounge pants and tank tops the rest of the week, I had made quite the transformation from a regular girl next door to vixen.

Damn, I look hot!

I took a cab to Vamps and experienced the familiar urge to bounce down the alley in anticipation for what lay ahead that night. I practically threw open the big door at the entrance.

Byron smiled widely. "Maya, Maya, Maya. You're back."

"Hi, Byron. How's it going?"

"Things have been—interesting," he said. "Someone was asking about you."

My heart beat faster and I tried to control my excitement. After all, it could be some random guy.

I tried for nonchalance. "Oh really, who might that be?"

He cocked his head. "Come on, Maya. Don't play coy."

"I don't know what on earth you mean, Byron." I opened my eyes wide for an innocent effect.

"Save it, sunshine. I'm gay, remember? Womanly wiles don't have any effect on me."

My wide-eyed look immediately was replaced by a pout, without me even realizing what I was doing.

"What's up with you and Mr. Stone anyway? "Byron asked.

Yes, it was him! He asked about me. I mentally jumped in the air clicking my heels like some kind of leprechaun. Then said, "Nothing. Why do you ask?"

"Mr. Stone is one of the most introverted people I've ever met. He stays down in his office or whatever he has downstairs and just sweeps through the club like a bat out of hell to make sure everything's going okay. Don't tell him, but that's what the staff calls him behind his back."

"Bat out of hell?"

"Yes. He scared the crap out of one of the bar help one day, who was replenishing the bottles behind the bar. Mr. Stone came up to check on things and he was wearing his usual black. He flew through the club and then he disappeared downstairs. That's how he usually acts. He does not talk to women and he does not take their hands to give them private tours of the club, like he did with you."

"Uh, um, oh," I stammered. "Maybe he was just being polite because you knew me."

"Maya, please. Why would the owner of a club care who the bouncer is friendly with?"

"Um." Good point. I had nothing.

"Exactly." He nodded as if thinking to himself. "He wants me to tell him when you return. You okay with that?"

Okay with that? I was hoping that he'd at least remember me. The fact that he asked about me and had given me special treatment made me want to spin some Olympic gymnastics flips off the rafters.

"Yeah, sure," I said with a wave of my hand, trying to play it cool. Then I killed that objective with my next line. "Byron, how do I look? Be honest."

Byron looked me over and a grin spread across his face again. "You look smashing. A total fox. If I was straight, I'd be all over you."

"Thanks," I said. "I'm going to get a drink. For some reason, I'm kind of nervous."

"You—nervous? First time for everything, I suppose," he said, shaking his head incredulously. "Go on in. I'll wait a little while before I tell him."

I went to the bar and checked out the drink list again. When I saw a Hotter Than Hell Bloody Mary, I smiled, remembering when Tristan suggested it. But there were so many new mouthwatering choices on the menu. What would I have next? I'm the type of girl who tries everything, not one who orders the same thing every time she goes to a restaurant.

"I'll have an Anything Goes," I told the sexy bartender.

Time to brace myself for anything that could happen.

A few songs later, Tristan hadn't appeared and I had almost finished my drink. Patience wasn't my strong suit, especially when it came to waiting for a guy.

Okay, maybe Byron got caught up at the door and didn't have a chance to tell him yet. Or maybe Tristan was caught up in something and wasn't going to stop everything and jump just because I walked into his club. Or maybe his interest had waned and he wasn't going to come up. The more I waited, the more my impatience grew.

Fuck it. I'm not going to wonder. I refuse to be that kind of girl. The kind who sits around making excuses waiting for some guy to show up. Vamps was my place to let loose and unwind from work, not get caught up in some romantic drama. Look at the toll this pining had taken on my psyche over the past couple of weeks. And for what? Nothing. Nothing but expectation, which did not look as if it was going to be met tonight.

Time to reclaim why I started to come here to begin with. To dance, to be free, to let the real me come out.

I walked out onto the dance floor and found a nook in the crowd that I made my own. It didn't take me long to get into the music. Forcing thoughts of Tristan aside, I lost myself into Billy Idol's *Flesh for Fantasy* mixed into some industrial track of a woman singing about her own fantasies. Then I made up for the last drab year of my life by dancing with wild abandon.

Tristan

When Byron called me to tell me that Maya was here, a part of me froze. I'd been waiting for her to return for days. But now that she was back—what the hell was I going to do?

Now I couldn't really go up to her and ask her probing questions about herself without setting off some red flags. Nor could I tell her about my abilities without her thinking I was some freak before she ran out the club never to turn back.

And I definitely couldn't tell her about that much more illicit thoughts that had crossed my mind since I'd met her.

Screw it. Perhaps that light was just a freak thing, someone might have slipped something into my drink. Maybe I'd go upstairs and she'd appear to me just like everyone else and whatever spell she'd cast on me would be broken.

Only one way to find out for sure.

I steeled myself and walked upstairs. Byron said she was at the bar. I walked up and down the bar, but didn't see her.

Had she already left?

I patrolled the perimeter of the dance floor. The sea of dancers dressed mostly in black were surrounded by that darkness only I could see. The dark auras moved so fast they looked fluid, like liquid shadows flowing around them.

And then I saw the light.

Maya dancing amid the darkness, her white light unmistakable, proving that last time was not a drug-induced vision or a hallucination. The darkness on the dance floor had disappeared, whether it was gone or I just couldn't see it anymore. People looked like people. Had she somehow chased it away?

She moved freely to the music, as if without a care as to what anyone around her thought. She faced away from me, but I knew it was her from the glow. She was wearing a black dress laced up the back with red. Wider openings in the top led to more narrow ones near the bottom as the fastenings cinched down near her waist and over her ass.

Seeing bits of her skin peek through the fastenings teased me. When my gaze travelled over the portion covering her ass, I pictured myself untying the red laces.

The song *Paralyzer* came on and she turned my way. When she danced, she moved as if one with the music. She raised her hands to the air while swaying her hips seductively, yet at the same time, not knowing the effect she had on her audience.

Which consisted of me. Utterly entranced.

Her free spirit was infectious. And her seductive moves were intoxicating. I couldn't take my eyes off her. Her face, those eyes, her curves in that dress, those long, long legs. Unable to resist her draw, I pushed my way through sweaty dancing bodies to get closer to her. Her back was toward me.

I tapped her shoulder and bent down to her ear. "Hello, Maya."

She froze. Then she turned back to look at me. Her midnight blue eyes shined like gems that reflected her light. It was my turn to freeze.

Paralyzed.

Although I'd always thought the song was hot, I also thought it was a little cheesy—falling for someone in a night-club? Come on. But now I felt the song as if it was written for this moment, for me and Maya. Who cared that maybe dozens of other people felt the same way about a partner they desired right now? For me, it was for Maya and me alone.

Recovering from the momentary stillness, I swayed across from her. I rarely danced, but something about the way Maya lost herself in the music convinced me to join her. Her mouth dropped halfway open, but after about two beats, she resumed dancing.

While we danced, our eyes remained locked. I became lost just gazing into those brilliant eyes. Spellbound. What was it about her that entranced me so?

Her brightness had faded to a pleasant glow, like a soft reading light. I remained fixated upon her, not even wanting or daring to look at anyone around us.

My desire for her overwhelmed rational thought at this point. I reached one hand around her lower back and pulled her closer to me. I admitted, "I've been thinking about you."

Her eyes fluttered and closed briefly in such an erotic gesture that I grew hard.

When she reopened them, she asked, "You have?"

I nodded. "Often." Then I grinned at a private joke. "You must have bewitched me."

"I'm no witch," she said, smiling back so brightly that her eyes twinkled. "Just a working girl who likes to dance."

"You do it so well."

"Thank you. Kudos to the DJ," she said, nodding in his direction.

Our bodies quickly synced as they swayed as one to the music I saw the want as her eyes darkened, a look that was surely reflected in my own. It was simply the most sensual dance of my life.

Maya rose onto tiptoes and moved closer to my ear. "I have a confession. I've been thinking about you too."

Surprised, I said, "Have you now?" When she nodded, I said. "All good things, I hope."

She looked down before looking back up with a mischievous look. "All good. And maybe a little bad. Or naughty."

Good God, did she know the effect those words just had on me?

She wrapped her arms around my neck, entwining them around me like a gorgeous serpentine. Just the feel of her arms around me was enough to make me want to moan.

"A naughty girl. Just what I like. And one who can dance as sexy as you."

"I dance sexy?" she asked, a confused look taking over the naughty glint.

"Almost too much for a man to bear," I said.

While we danced with our eyes still locked, I grew painfully aware of my growing erection just centimeters away from her luscious body. How I wanted to press myself against her, into her. People around us be damned. I wanted to throw her onto the floor and take her then and there.

No. I wanted to take my time with her. Take her down to my lab, explore every inch of her.

Surveying her body was a mistake. Her breasts were pushed up against the lace bodice and at my angle, I could see them at a great advantage. A deep groan escaped my lips. Luckily, it was drowned out by the song.

My eyes moved back up to her face. She was wearing such spiked heels that her face was mere inches away from mine. And her lips. She had painted them a sensual red. Now I couldn't take my eyes off her lips.

Then she licked them. Whether intentional or not, I don't know.

But I didn't stand a chance.

I didn't care who was around. Or that I owned this damn

LISA CARLISLE

club and had employees here working for me. I pulled her closer, so our bodies pressed against each other.

God, how I wanted to kiss her. I leaned in closer, shortening the space between us until they were less than an inch apart...

READ FIRE NOW!

READ MORE ABOUT the Underground Encounters series

ACKNOWLEDGMENTS

As always, I am so grateful to everyone who helps make each book possible, helping me shape the ideas in my head into a story. Huge thanks to my fellow authors, critique partners, editors, beta readers, ARC readers, Street Team, and you, the reader!

ABOUT THE AUTHOR

USA Today Bestselling author Lisa Carlisle loves stories with dark, brooding heroes and spirited heroines. She is thrilled to be a multi-published author since she's wanted to write since the sixth grade. Her travels and many jobs have provided her with inspiration for novels, such as deploying to Okinawa, Japan, backpacking alone around Europe, or working as a waitress in Paris. Her love of books inspired her to own a small independent book store for a couple of years. Lisa now lives in New England with her husband, children, two kittens, and many fish.

Sign up for her VIP list to hear about new releases, specials, and freebies:

www.lisacarlislebooks.com/subscribe/

Visit her website for more on books, trailers, playlists, and more:

Lisacarlislebooks.com

Lisa loves to connect with readers. You can find her on:

Facebook
Twitter - @lisacbooks
Pinterest
Instagram
Goodreads

Knights of Stone: Mason

Highland Gargoyles 1

A Romance Reviews Top Pick!

Few have ever dared to cross the boundaries--until now...

With a quarter century of burning hatred between the inhabitants of the Isle of Stone, Kayla knows all too well it is forbidden to cross boundaries. But that doesn't keep her from being sorely tempted.

Drawn to discover the secrets beyond the tree witches' forest, Kayla is intrigued by the talk of unconventional rock concerts in gargoyle territory.

But when she risks everything to sneak away from the coven, she never expects to return night after night, not just for the music, but for one particular gargoyle who captured her heart with his guitar.

Nor did she expect that her attention had not gone unnoticed...

With plans to seduce the pixie-like female, Mason spent several nights keeping a watchful eye on his prize, unaware she's not just a passing visitor. But when he discovers she's a tree witch, an enemy to his entire kind, Mason knows that anything between them would be forbidden. No matter how strong the temptation...

But other elements command their attention.

Something much more dangerous haunts the wolf shifters of the isle....

With the magic veil thinning there will be blood... and the full moon is coming.

Knights of Stone: Mason is the first book in a shifter paranormal romance series with a Highland touch and a hard hit of rock romance. If you like hot men in kilts, dark paranormal thrills, and forbidden love, then you'll be hooked by the Highland Gargoyles Series!

Other books in the Highland Gargoyles series:

- **Knights of Stone: Mason**
- **Knights of Stone: Lachlan**
- **Knights of Stone: Bryce**
- **Seth - a wolf shifter romance in the series**
- **Knights of Stone: Calum**

Chateau Seductions, a Paranormal Erotic Romance Series

Darkness Rising

Antoine Chevalier harbors a secret. Born a gargoyle shifter, he wants nothing more than to cultivate his art. His hard work pays off the night he completes his greatest sculpture. But the excitement of his accomplishment doesn't last.

He's drawn the eye of the wrong group—a clan of vampires. Antoine wakes into darkness, changed. Shattered. His dream of becoming a renowned sculptor is destroyed.

One question remains—how will he ever survive an eternity of darkness alone?

Darkness Rising is part 0.5 of the Chateau Seductions series by USA Today Bestselling author Lisa Carlisle. Readers have requested more on the dark and mysterious Antoine. In this short story, Antoine tells his tale, which continues in the series with Dark Velvet. Dark Velvet is written from Savannah's perspective as a newcomer to an art colony who is intrigued by the proprietor.

Read Now!

Dark Velvet

Grad student Savannah Evans is thrilled to be accepted as a resident to a prestigious art colony. Where else would she be able to focus on her craft of writing poetry in a setting like that of the medieval-styled castle? The remote New England island is a respite from her hectic city life. When she meets her benefactor, a mysterious French sculptor, her expectations for carefree days writing near the ocean are distracted by unprofessional fantasies about her sponsor.

Antoine Chevalier built Les Beaux Arts on DeRoche Island to bring purpose back to an existence that has lost meaning. He's wandered the earth for decades and finds solace in returning to art. When Savannah applies for a residency, something about her words touches him. After her arrival, a physical attraction grows between them, which he struggles against. She deserves more than someone of his kind.

Antoine proposes they become lovers during her stay. But the situation turns complicated when Savannah discovers his secret. She had suspicions about his identity, but finds the truth overwhelming. Consumed by her desire for Antoine and faced with a tough decision, she is blind to the danger that has arrived at DeRoche Island.

"Dark Velvet has a dark eroticism that makes you want to be Savannah. It is a book that is a good, quick and darkly thrilling read." ~ Books and Beyond Fifty Shades

"...insanely hot chemistry between the female protagonist Savannah & vampire Antoine. Their intensity starts off right away and you're not a chapter in before it takes off like a rocket!" ~ Paranormal Romance Junkies

Read Now!

Dark Muse

It takes time before Gina Meiro warms up to people and her shyness is often misunderstood. She hasn't had to worry about meeting new people at a remote art colony until a new resident arrives—a rock guitarist more suited for a billboard. Her carefree days of painting at the medieval-styled castle on a remote New England island are shattered when she stumbles right into his welcome gathering.

After a falling out with his band, Dante Riani wants nothing more at Les Beaux Arts on DeRoche Island than solitude to work on new songs. When a shy young painter asks to paint him at sunset, he's tempted by the opportunity to be alone with her.

Someone at the colony claims to know what Dante is and asks for his help. Dante fears his plans are coming undone, especially as grows more drawn to Gina. Her scent and vulnerability are too difficult to resist. But he must stay away from her—she would never understand his secret.

While it is a story about struggle, it is also about love; and doing whatever needs to be done to be with the one you are attracted to. I really enjoyed the dynamic between Gina and Dante. This story has the perfect amount of witty banter, sex, and romance."

Read Now!

Dark Stranger

Wolf shifters come to Chateau seeking a missing pack member. During an altercation, Cameron Stevens, the manager of the art colony, is separated from the others. He ends up alone with Nadya, one of the female shifters.

Together, in the forests of DeRoche Island, they struggle against conflicting feelings. In addition to battling each other as well as their mistrust, they fight a powerful, inexplicable attraction to one another—one that leaves them irrevocably entwined.

They're mates? Cameron can't comprehend or accept such a thing is possible. They're two different species and their worlds don't mesh. He can't fight the heated desire burning between them and her touch is impossible to resist. His heart and mind aren't on the same page where she's concerned. One thing is certain—Nadya is stamped on both.

***** FIVE STARS ***** – "I have read the first 2 books in this series and could not wait to get my hands on this one; and I was not disappointed. The thing I love most, is that while this is a story about paranormal creatures, you can still relate to the trial and tribulations that they go through. You can relate to how each character is feeling, even though you are nothing like them."

~ Books and Beyond Fifty Shades

Read Now!

Temptation Returns

Antonio returns from the Marine Corps to begin a new life as a civilian. While visiting Cape Cod, he meets a strange woman who reads his Tarot cards. He doesn't believe in such nonsense; after all, he's a Marine. When he returns to Boston, he receives a ticket to a rock club where he runs into the one woman he never forgot.

Lina can't believe Antonio is back in town, right before her wedding. Being around him again resurrects long-buried feelings. Will she be able to resist temptation in the form of a dark-haired Italian Marine, the same man who once broke her heart?

4.5 Hearts from Books and Bindings

"This saucy little story hit the spot with interesting characters, some humor, some spice, and a thoughtful NA second chance love story about a returning vet with a few issues."

"I enjoyed the story, humor, and steam – oh yeah, did I mention the spice? Let's mention it again just to be safe."

Read Now!

Dress Blues

Sometimes it all comes down to timing...

Volunteering at a cat shelter is much calmer than the adrenaline-fueled skirmishes of Vivi Parker's last deployment in the Marines, but her limp is a constant reminder of what she endured. The shelter is her sanctuary, her one relief from memories that haunt her. At a fundraiser, she runs into a man she could never have while she served, but had never forgotten.

Active duty had its challenges, but starting over as a civilian in Boston is more difficult than Jack Conroy anticipated. When his mom and sister drag him to a cat benefit, he never expects to see a woman he last saw in Dress Blues--a woman he couldn't have, but could never forget.

Vivi fears she's no longer the woman Jack was drawn to, able to tackle rock climbing walls or other outdoor challenges. And Jack has decisions he must face.

Military rules forbade their burgeoning passion. But now, years later, the rules have changed.

Yet, so have they.

Is it ever too late for a second chance at love?

"Wow! Dress Blues is an awesome, fun, short must read in contemporary romantic fiction with a side of hot military characters and some sweet, fuzzy furballs!"

"An amazing story of two damaged Marines finding each other again."

"This is a fun, furry, feel good story of second chances... Ms. Carlisle's writing style grabs you from the first word and keeps you engaged with witty banter and sexy scenes. I loved this short second chance romance with a HEA and I'm sure you will too!"

Read Now!

Pursued

A Vampire Blood Courtesans Romance

A Night Owl Reviews Top Pick!

It was only meant to be three nights...

After watching my mother die, becoming a Blood Courtesan is key to my future in medicine. With loans racking up, all I have to do is pretend I want the money for tuition, and I'm hired. **No one can know the real reason for wanting this job.**

But it isn't as easy as it first seems. On my first night as a courtesan at a ball in Salem, I meet vampires for the first time--and flee.

Vampires are not easily dissuaded. And one in particular, Renato, offers me a proposal I find difficult to resist. He has a dark, smoldering appeal that lures me in. Plus, I might gain the insight I seek.

I'm supposed to provide a service and will be paid well for it. **But my feelings complicate our arrangement--and endanger my life.**

It was only meant to be three nights, but can I walk away now?

Welcome to the shadow world of Blood Courtesans...where vampires are real and blood is a commodity.

It's not supposed to be about love...until it is.

PURSUED is part of the Blood Courtesan series, starting with REBORN, Myra's story. See the full list of books here: bloodcourtesans.com.

Read Now!

When Darkness Whispers

A Romance Reads Top Pick!

Some memories are better left forgotten...

Haunted by an unclear past, biologically enhanced Marine, Eva

Montreaux, can't be distracted from her mission. With American servicemen being brutally murdered on the island of Okinawa, it's more than priority. It's critical. But when her investigation brings her face to face with Marcos Delacruz, it triggers memories. Ones she lost. Memories that somehow include him.

Marcos Delacruz has tried to forget the woman who left him with nothing but empty promises. Even now, three years later, Eva doesn't seem to express any guilt over breaking his heart. In truth, she seems to barely recognize him. This deployment has been challenging enough with too many restless spirits haunting the island. But when his own investigation forces him to cross paths with her once more, Marcos discovers there may be a deeper truth.

With the number of murders climbing rapidly and the rising need to track the murderer across the tropical island, Eva struggles to reclaim what she lost. But the island holds darker elements--a serial killer. One that doesn't appear to be human.

Thrust into a world she can't escape, Eva must discover a way to stop a murderer from destroying anyone else's future, but how can she succeed if she can't even remember what role Marcos played in her past?

When Darkness Whispers is full of paranormal romantic suspense you won't want to put down! Go undercover with a supernatural team into a world of vampires, gargoyles, shifters, demons, and ghosts. If you like haunting mystery, spine-tingling suspense, and Japanese mythology, you'll love When Darkness Whispers!

"Wow If I could give this story more than 5 stars I would... Suspense, Mystery, and Thrills all in one book." ~ *Book Nook Nuts*

Read Now!

Visit lisacarlislebooks.com for the latest releases, news, book trailers, and more!

74129412R00090

Made in the USA
Middletown, DE
20 May 2018